# FIREFLIES & FAMILY TIES

RACHEL HANNA

# FOREWORD

Thank you for picking up FIREFLIES & FAMILY TIES!

   I would also like to offer a FREE January Cove book to you as well! Just click on the image below to download your copy of WAITING FOR YOU.

# CHAPTER 1

*J*anine stood in the middle of the open space, only the sound of William's expensive dress shoes tapping the hardwood floors as the sound echoed all around them.

"It's so big," she said, looking at the wall of mirrors in front of her.

William walked up behind her and put his hands on her shoulders. "And you're going to fill all of this space easily," he said, planting a kiss on her cheek. "Think of all the classes you can have here."

"Are you sure I'm not moving too fast? I mean, this place has monthly rent I'll need to pay, and honestly I've never been that good at accounting. How will I keep up with all the numbers?"

Janine had spent most of her adult life traveling the globe, teaching yoga and meditation at different retreats. This was the first time she would be the one in charge, and ultimately, the one responsible. Failure was a very big possibility in her mind, and the thought terrified her.

William turned her around and looked at her. "You're a rockstar, honey. You need room to grow. Look at all the people you've already helped in the last few weeks. Yoga is your gift."

"I wish I had as much confidence in myself as you do," she said, grinning as she looked up at him.

Their relationship had blossomed a lot faster than she had anticipated. William, often an outsider himself, had just "gotten" her. They had an ease with each other, and it was something she hadn't experienced with anyone else.

"Well, I do have confidence in you. And I'll help you however I need to. This is your dream, Janine. I think the universe is giving you a sign."

She scrunched her nose at him. "Don't you use the universe against me. You know I fall for anything I think is universe related."

"My woo woo girlfriend," he said, rolling his eyes and laughing.

"Girlfriend?" They hadn't made anything official, at least not out loud. He froze for a moment. Slowly, a slight smile spread across his face.

"Did I misread our… situation?"

"No, of course not," she said, smiling as she

closed the distance between them and put her hands on his chest. "I've just never heard you refer to me that way before."

He slid his arms around her waist and pulled her closer. "My *girlfriend* is so cute."

"My *boyfriend* is equally adorable," she said, touching her nose to his.

"My *sister* is grossing me out," Julie said from the doorway. Janine and William broke apart, each of their faces turning red.

"What are you doing here?" Janine asked, nervously laughing.

"You invited me to see the place, remember? Or are the endorphins affecting your memory?"

William and Janine laughed. "Sorry. We were just…"

"Sis, it's okay. I'm happy for both of you," Julie said, rubbing Janine's arm. "As for this place… I love it!"

"You do?"

"It's absolutely perfect for you. And right on the square? These kinds of properties never come up for rent. And for the price? You have to do this!"

"Thank you," William said under his breath.

"I think it's one of those signs from the universe you like so much."

Janine chuckled. "Somebody else said the same thing."

"Well?" William said, his eyes wide as he waited for her answer.

"I'm going to do it!" Janine squealed as she jumped up and down with excitement. "And I'm completely freaked out!"

∾

MEG STARED at herself in the mirror, something she did several times a day. It was getting harder and harder to keep her secret from her mother, sister and aunt. Twice, she'd caught her aunt Janine staring at her, as if she was trying to figure out what was different.

Always petite, Meg had been able to hide her growing belly for the past few weeks since arriving at her mother's new house on Seagrove Island. But she couldn't do that forever. A baby was growing inside of her, and each day her midsection expanded a little more.

She turned to see another angle, hoping the over-sized sweatshirt she was wearing would keep her secret for another day. In all honesty, she didn't know why she was still keeping it a secret anyway. She'd have to tell her mother at some point, but the thought of disappointing her was too much to handle in her fragile emotional state.

What would her mother think of her? Nineteen

and pregnant. Unmarried. No boyfriend. Left college. Ugh, this wasn't what she had planned when she left for Europe all those months ago.

Today was an important day. Although she had seen a doctor a few times in France, she was eager to see a new OBGYN. Making sure her baby was healthy was the most important thing right now. Even though she hadn't made any decisions about whether she was keeping the baby or pursuing adoption, she wanted to give it the best shot at a healthy start in life.

Almost five months along, she was hoping to learn the sex today. She touched up her minimal makeup - she'd never been into that kind of stuff, preferring a much simpler look - and walked out the front door. The car she'd called hadn't pulled up yet, so she sat down on the top step and stared out into the front yard. Never in a million years would she have expected her mother to settle in a place like this.

The house was cute enough, but the marshland could be a bit scary. At any moment, she expected an alligator to saunter up and have her for lunch. But, it was peaceful here, and it was one of the better places she could think of to hide out from life's twists and turns.

"Going somewhere?"

She turned, startled, and saw Janine sitting at the

end of the porch, her bare feet gently guiding the wooden porch swing back and forth.

Meg put her hand to her chest. "Good Lord, Aunt Janine! You just about gave me a heart attack!"

Janine smiled. "Sorry. I am known for my ninja-like qualities."

"Why are you lurking over there? I thought you had to sign some papers for your new yoga studio today?"

"That's later this afternoon. And you didn't answer my question, young lady," she said as she walked over and sat down next to her niece. Meg pressed her forehead to her knees, something that was getting harder to do by the day.

"Just going into town for some supplies." Lying had never been her forte, which was why she was keeping her head down and her eyes away from Janine's.

"Do you think I just fell off the turnip truck?"

Meg looked at her. "What do you mean?"

"I know you're pregnant, sweetie."

Meg's stomach churned, and she couldn't distinguish whether it was nerves or her lingering morning sickness. "What?"

"You can be honest with me, hon. I promise."

Meg sucked in a long, deep breath and blew it out slowly. "Who else knows?"

"No one. At least, I don't think so. Your mother's

been so busy these days with work and Colleen coming home that I don't think she's noticed... yet. But, she will, Meg. Why are you keeping this a secret?"

A stray tear ran down Meg's face. Keeping the secret had worn her down in ways she couldn't describe, and now that someone else knew, she felt a bit of the weight release from her shoulders.

"I don't want to disappoint my mother," she squeaked out, tears now flowing freely down her cheeks. Janine put her arm around Meg's shoulders and pulled her close.

"Now, you stop saying things like that! Your mother is proud of you and always will be."

"I'm nineteen, pregnant and a college dropout. I'm sure she'll be thrilled to share all of that with her friends."

Janine chuckled. "Well, I don't think those were high on her list of hopes and dreams for you, no."

"Thanks a lot," Meg said, sitting back up and putting her forehead onto her knees again.

"Sweetie, your mother adores you. And while this is a bump in the road, she'll be there for you no matter what. She will love you and that little bundle of joy. She's going to be so excited to be a grandma..."

"Stop. Please." Meg held up her hand as if she couldn't take hearing another word.

"What?"

Meg looked at her. "I don't know if I'm keeping the baby."

Janine stared at her like she didn't understand English. "Oh, Meg, you can't…"

"Please don't say anything. This is already hard enough. I just can't take much more."

Janine hugged her again. "I'm sorry. I know this must be so much stress on you, sweetie. But, I want you to know I'm here for you. No matter what. And I want to take you to your appointment."

"How did you know about my appointment?"

"I should've been an FBI agent," Janine said with a laugh. "Plus, the walls in this place are incredibly thin. I heard you confirm your appointment on the phone yesterday."

"I never expected my life to end up like this," Meg lamented, putting her face in her hands.

Janine rubbed her shoulder. "This isn't the end of the world, Meg. Things like this happen. Life throws us curveballs."

"This is a baby, Aunt Janine. A human life. So much responsibility. I mean, last year I was picking out my prom dress and now I'm going to get an ultrasound of a small human being growing inside of my body!" She stood up and started pacing back and forth on the porch. "How am I going to tell Mom about this?"

Janine stood and stopped Meg from walking, putting her hands on Meg's shoulders. "You're not alone. You know that, right?"

Meg nodded slightly, her eyes puffy and red. "I know."

"Now, let's take things one step at a time and go to your appointment first. Then we can talk about what the doctor says. Okay?"

"Okay," Meg said, letting out a deep breath she'd been holding. "Where's the car I called anyway?"

Janine chuckled. "I may have cancelled it."

COLLEEN STARED out of her office window. Readjusting to life after a breakup hadn't been easy, and doing it in a small town had been just as jarring. Not that she didn't love her new island oasis; she just didn't know how to keep herself busy.

Life in California had been much more of a frantic pace. The law firm where she'd worked had cases stacked a mile high, and she was able to immerse herself in facts and figures when her heart was hurting. Truth be told, she'd known Peter wasn't the man she'd dreamed about since she was a little girl. All those times she and Meg had donned white pillow cases on their heads and marched around their bedroom, dreaming of Prince

Charming coming to whisk them away in a magic carriage.

Peter hadn't been Prince Charming.

Still, she was finding life lonely. She loved being near her family again, but not having someone to hold her tight after a hard day at work was tougher than she had anticipated. Working with domestic violence cases all day was draining. She'd already seen things she couldn't get out of her mind, and she wanted to help every single person - women and children, mostly. Although she was only pushing paperwork around and not actually representing anyone, she felt responsible for them all. She wanted to make a difference more than anything in the world.

Meeting Peter had stolen that from her. He was back in California, probably dating another unsuspecting woman with low self-esteem. For now, she was going to work on herself. On her career. No more men, at least not for a few years. That was what she told herself even as she avoided eye contact with a man she'd just met in town. He walked past her window, which faced the sidewalk leading to the square, and waved.

Why was he so handsome? But not just regular handsome. He was Southern hunk movie-star handsome. His walk was easy, not cocky. His smile was like a lazy Sunday afternoon in a hammock. Tall, dark and handsome had nothing on this guy.

"Wow, who was that?" Candace asked from behind her. Candace was a new temp who was helping to organize files for a huge case the firm was taking on.

Colleen looked up and chuckled. "I know, right? He's pretty… well, he's actually pretty. Like, I'm jealous he's prettier than me."

Candace laughed. "He's gorgeous, like some kind of live model for a marble sculpture. Do you know him?"

"Not really. I met him when I was in line to get coffee the other day. His name is Tucker."

"Yum. Tucker. That fits perfectly. I just want to pinch his cheeks, and I'm not even talking about the ones on his face."

Colleen swept her hand up and smacked Candace's arm. "Get back to work. You're drooling on my shoulder."

Candace laughed as she walked back to her desk. Colleen checked to make sure she wasn't looking and then leaned toward her window to get one final look at Tucker as he walked down the sidewalk.

DAWSON REACHED high above the window and screwed the rod into place. He stepped off the ladder and sucked in a deep breath.

"I thought I was in good shape," he said, laughing.

"You're in much better shape than I am. Why do men age so well, and women have to worry about things sagging and drooping?" Julie said.

He walked toward her, cupping her cheeks in his hands. "You, my dear, are certainly not sagging or drooping. You're stunningly smart and beautiful, a deadly combination."

Her insides melted. What had she done to deserve a man like this? On his best days, Michael had never said anything close to that. The best he'd done was "I'll still love you even if you get fat one day". And then when she'd had trouble losing weight after Meg was born, he'd given her a gift card to a nutritionist for Christmas.

After planting another memorable kiss on her lips, Dawson stepped back and looked around the room. "I think Granny would love it."

"You do? I hope so. I'm no interior decorator but I tried to find pieces that would work with the time period."

For the last couple of weeks, Dawson and Julie had been redecorating the living room of his house. Dark and dusty, it needed an update, but they both wanted to keep it in line with the time period.

"I couldn't have done this without you," he said, putting his arm around her as they looked around the room together. "My Granny would've loved you."

"You think so?"

"I know so. Granny was a good judge of character. You couldn't get anything past her. She was only four-foot-ten, but she stood twenty feet tall when she walked in a room. Grandpa was six-foot-five and terrified of her."

Julie laughed. "I wish I had gotten to meet her."

"Me too."

"So, I've been wanting to ask you something."

"Okay. What's up?"

"My high school reunion is Saturday night. I was wondering if you'd like to be my date?"

Julie grinned. "Really? You want to take me… the *older* woman?"

"You're three years older than me," he said with a laugh.

"But won't that ruin your rep?"

He slid his arms around her waist. "And what rep is that?"

"I bet you were every girl's dream date in high school."

"Not even close. I was a tall, dorky mess. I was always surprised that Tania even paid attention to me."

Julie smiled. "I'm sure she felt blessed to have a man like you, Dawson."

"Well, I hope she felt that way," he said, pulling back a bit.

"Who else did you date in high school?"

"Tania and I didn't meet until senior year. Before that, I was pretty much a free agent. I did have a crush though."

"Oh yeah?" she said, poking him in the side.

"Every guy in school was in love with this girl named Tiffany."

"I'm convinced that every Tiffany is popular, has a platinum blonde ponytail and is head cheerleader."

Dawson smiled. "You hit the nail on the head. And every guy walked around our high school with their tongues hanging out. But, Tiffany would have none of it. She finally ended up with the captain of the football team, Blaine."

"Tiffany and Blaine? Sounds like something out of a bad eighties movie."

Dawson nodded. "It was. They were Ken and Barbie. I think they got married right out of high school. Last I heard, Blaine was running an insurance agency out of Austin, Texas."

"And Tiffany?"

"I have no idea. Probably getting spray tans and doing aerobics somewhere."

"Maybe she'll be at the reunion," Julie said, playfully.

"Doubtful, but I'll only have eyes for you so I won't notice."

He pulled her into a warm embrace, kissing the top of her head, and Julie decided time could stand still forever and she'd be just fine.

# CHAPTER 2

eg couldn't remember a time she'd felt more nervous. As she sat there in her little paper gown, which was covering less of her these days, she dangled her legs over the edge of the table. Doctor Hodges was supposed to be the best of the best. All of her online research had shown him to be reputable, so driving over to Charleston hadn't been too much to ask.

"Are you okay?" Janine asked again.

"Yes, why?"

"Because you're flinging your legs so hard that I'm afraid you might take flight in a minute."

"Sorry. I'm a nervous wreck. I hate… feminine… exams. I'd only ever been to the gynecologist once… before all of this."

"Sweetie, it's going to be okay. This is a nice

office, and I checked out the doc's medical degrees in the hallway. He seems top notch."

"Gosh, if Mom knew where I was right now…"

"One thing at a time, remember?"

Meg nodded her head just as the doctor opened the door, a nurse following closely behind him. He was short and rounder than she expected, a tuft of gray hair atop his head. But, he had a warm smile, and that settled her down a bit.

"Miss Pike?" he said, reaching out his hand to shake hers.

"That's me. Meg. And this is my Aunt Janine."

"Nice to meet you both. I've read your file, and I understand the circumstances. I know this is an emotional time for you, so I want you to know you can ask me any questions. What we're going to do first is an ultrasound so we can see your baby's growth."

"Okay."

Meg laid back against the table as the nurse set up the ultrasound machine. Within minutes, she was staring into the small monitor looking at her baby. No longer did it look like some mutant blob. Now, it was a small baby, and she almost wished she hadn't seen it. Adoption had been a real option since she learned she was pregnant, but could she really give up her child?

"Now, here's the baby's head up here…" the

doctor said as the nurse moved the wand around. They took measurements here and there, but Meg heard little of what he said.

"Is the baby… healthy?"

"Everything looks right on track. You're right at eighteen weeks along. Now, we can see the sex of the baby if you'd like to know."

Meg's heart skipped a beat. Did she want to know? Wouldn't that make it more real?

"Oh, Meg, don't you want to know?" Janine chimed in from the corner of the room.

She swallowed hard. "I don't want to know. At least, not right now. Can you put it in a sealed envelope for me?"

She glanced at Janine, who looked a little sad. She quickly perked up when she realized Meg was looking at her.

"Of course. Here, take these paper towels and clean off all that goo while we get these pictures printed out for you."

Meg wiped her belly and sat up, tossing the wad of paper towels across the room and completely missing the trashcan. She never was all that great at basketball.

"Are you taking any prenatal vitamins?" the nurse asked.

"Yes, I have been. But, I just ran out."

"Okay, we can give you some that we recommend here."

"You'll need to come back in two weeks," the doctor said, as he continued noting her chart. "You can make an appointment with Clara at the front desk. Any questions?"

Meg took in a deep breath and blew it out slowly. "Yes. Do you know of a good adoption agency?"

"THIS ONE OR THIS ONE?" Julie asked as she held up two very different dresses. One was a basic black cocktail dress while the other was a sexier red number that would likely turn heads when she walked into Dawson's reunion.

"Well, darlin', call me old fashioned, but I think that red one might make you look like you're advertising something you aren't selling," Dixie said in her normal honest fashion.

Julie laughed. "Too much?"

"Just a tad."

"I just want to look good for Dawson's reunion," she said as she laid both dresses over the counter. The bookstore had been slow since Christmas, but Dixie didn't seem concerned. She said it always ebbed and flowed and encouraged Julie to enjoy the down time before the tourism season kicked into high gear in the spring.

"Dear, you're gonna look gorgeous no matter what you do," Dixie said as she sauntered over to the cash register. Since her Parkinson's medications were working well, her saunter had once again replaced her slower, shuffling gait. Julie was thrilled at how she had responded to her medication and physical therapy treatments so far. She wanted to keep Dixie spry and active for as long as possible.

"Good afternoon, ladies," Janine said as she walked into the bookstore. She looked exhausted, and Julie couldn't even remember the last time they sat down and had a meal together. With her new yoga studio getting ready to open and Meg showing up in town, things had been hectic to say the least.

"Hey, Janine," Dixie said, throwing up her hand. "How's the studio coming along?"

Janine sat down in the overstuffed armchair near the historical romance section and then flung her head over between her legs, her thick mane of curls dangling precariously close to the terra-cotta floor.

"Is there a problem?" Julie asked.

"There are nothing but problems. William found a leak in the ceiling right above the practice room. The landlord is giving me problems with the rental agreement changes I wanted to make. My flyers went out with the wrong address. And," she said, sitting up and sighing, "I think I pulled my adductor longus."

"Your what now?" Dixie asked, leaning on the counter, her snazzy leopard print reading glasses balancing on the tip of her nose.

"My inner thigh muscle. I was trying to show off a bit to William, and, well, I pulled it. How am I going to teach classes next week with a pulled groin and water falling on my head from the ceiling?" She put her head back between her knees and groaned.

"You were showing William what, exactly?" Julie asked.

Janine sat up and rolled her eyes. "A yoga pose. Get your head out of the gutter. His Mom is right there, for goodness sakes!" she whispered loudly.

"Oh, now, come on, Janine. Everything's gonna be just fine. My boy knows how to fix a leak. He had to do a lot of that when he was a kid. Johnny taught him everything a man should know."

"Or a woman," Julie whispered to her sister.

"Well, call me an old timer, but I think men should know certain things. How to change a tire, take out the trash, kill the biggest bugs this side of the Mississippi…"

Janine smiled. "Dixie, you crack me up sometimes."

"But, she's right, sis. Everything will work out fine. I'll help you get the flyers fixed, and I'm sure

Dawson will help us get them distributed again. And I can talk to your landlord if you need me to."

"Let me have a chat with old Clarence. We've known each other for decades, and he sure doesn't want to mess around with me," Dixie said, standing upright and crossing her arms.

"I appreciate it, Dixie, but I should handle it. I wouldn't want him to think I'm a pushover. People tend to assume that I am because I do yoga."

"Well, if you need me, you know where to find me." Dixie walked out from behind the register. "Now, if you ladies will excuse me, I've got a lunch date with a certain someone."

"Ohhh, do tell," Julie said, grinning. Dixie waved her hand in the air and walked out the front door, laughing the whole way.

After she left, Julie stood up and started unpacking books from a new shipment that had arrived earlier in the day. She loved the smell of books, new or old. It made her feel comforted, like all those times she was a kid and got a new book at the school book fair. It was her favorite day of the school year, and her mother always gave her a fresh, crisp ten dollar bill to spend. She always felt bad for the kids who didn't have any money to spend, so she often ended up sharing it with one of them.

"Say, have you seen Meg today?" Julie asked.

Janine cleared her throat. "No, why?"

"I was just wondering. I left early this morning, and I kind of expected her to stop by. She still hasn't seen the bookstore."

"Really? Well, I'm sure she's just getting readjusted to life stateside. Besides, that plane ride must've been a doozy as far as jet lag."

Julie laughed. "That was a couple of weeks ago. I think the jet lag would've worn off by now."

"Right. Well, I'd better get back to the studio. The sign guy is coming this afternoon, and I'm praying at least that much works out."

"It will all work out, sis. You're going to do great things here." Julie pulled her sister into a hug.

"I'm glad you've got my back," Janine said.

"Always."

Janine walked toward the door, but turned back to her sister. "Hey, Julie?"

"Yeah?"

She paused for a long moment. "You know I'd never do anything to hurt you, right?"

Julie cocked her head to the side. "Of course. Why do you ask that?"

Janine smiled slightly. "I just want you to know I always have your back too."

~

MEG SAT in front of the attorney, her palms sweating in her disappearing lap. It had only been a few days since her OBGYN appointment, and her mind had been swirling with thoughts. What should she do?

In her heart, she didn't want to give up her baby. But what choice did she have? She wanted the best for her child, and being a single mother starting over with no education or job didn't seem like the best start to life for a kid.

On the other hand, she knew her family would help her. She had resources. But was it fair to ask her family to help her out of the situation she found herself in?

"Miss Pike? Did you hear me?"

"What? I'm sorry, Mr. Richter. I zoned out for a moment. Pregnancy is causing a little brain fog lately."

He smiled graciously. "Understandable. I was just saying that you have a choice between private and open adoption. Most folks do choose open adoption these days. That would be where you'd get some photos over the years, but some families want more contact than that. Really depends on the situation."

"Oh. I don't know if I could do that."

He looked at her quizzically. "You wouldn't want to see pictures of the baby as he or she grew up?"

Her stomach knotted up, and she struggled to keep tears from falling down her cheeks. "I'm not sure I could see pictures and not want to go get my child."

Her honesty seemed to surprise him. "You can't change your mind, Miss Pike. Once the adoption papers are signed, that's it. South Carolina doesn't have laws like some states do, you know, for a reflection period."

"A reflection period?"

"To change your mind and get your child back. South Carolina has no such laws. You need to be sure about your decision because there's no going back."

"I'm just not sure…"

"No pressure, dear. You have plenty of time to think about it. But I will say you want to make a decision over the next month or so, just to give yourself time to review adoptive parent files."

All of it seemed to be too much. Doing this alone at only nineteen years old was weighing on Meg. For her whole life, she'd dreamed of meeting her knight in shining armor, getting married in a lavish affair with doves and flying handfuls of rice, and riding off into her new perfect life. She'd planned to have at least three kids, live near the ocean and serve on every committee at her kids' school.

How would she do that now? How would she ever look her other children in their precious little eyes and tell them that she gave their sibling away to strangers? How would God ever bless her with more kids if she didn't even care enough to keep this one?

"Are you okay?" Mr. Richter asked.

Meg couldn't catch her breath. She put her hand to her chest and felt the pounding of her heart. Sweat beaded on her brow, and her hands shook. "I… can't… breathe…"

"Karen, get Miss Pike some water," he called down the hallway. He sat down in the chair beside her and put his hand on her shoulder. An older man, she imagined he must be someone's grandfather, and she could sure use that kind of energy right now.

His secretary, Karen, ran into the room with a bottle of water. Mr. Richter opened it and handed it to her. She lifted it to her mouth and took a long sip, trying to get her heart to stop pounding in her ears.

"Have you ever had a panic attack, hon?" Karen asked.

Meg nodded her head. "A couple of times, but never quite this bad. Thanks for the water."

"Maybe we should take you to the ER?" Mr. Richter said.

"No!" she said a little too forcefully. The last thing she wanted was for her mother to find out where she was. She needed a little more time. Maybe one day it would feel right to tell her. "I'm fine. Or at least I will be. I think I just need to go home, put my feet up and have a snack."

"Are you able to drive?"

"I've got a car picking me up, actually."

"Let Karen drive you. I wouldn't feel right putting you in a car with a stranger after all of this."

"It's really fine."

"Miss Pike, I've got a legal obligation. Please just humor me, okay?"

She smiled. "Okay. But it's really not necessary. I feel a lot better already."

They helped her up and out to Karen's car. She was exhausted. Nights of not sleeping, worried over what her mother and sister were going to think of her, were starting to wear her down.

They drove in silence for a few moments, but Meg could see Karen glancing at her over and over. She seemed to be a nice woman, probably about her mother's age, with black hair and a very pronounced nose.

"I know this isn't easy, especially for a girl your age," she said as she turned down the main road that would lead back toward the island.

"It's definitely not."

"I'm not supposed to do this, but can I give you a little motherly advice?"

"Of course," Meg said, softly. She wasn't about to tell the woman that she just wanted a quiet ride and no unsolicited advice.

"Really listen to your heart. This is a lifelong decision, and it's one you don't want to regret."

"I just want to do what's best for this baby."

"Which might just show what a good mother you already are," she said, smiling at her. They pulled onto the island and she stopped just short of Julie's house.

"What's going on?"

"I just want to say that it takes a lot of bravery for you to even consider adoption. There are some amazing people out there who can't have kids, and women like you make that dream happen for them. However…"

"However?"

"There are also some brave young women who consider adoption, but ultimately make the decision to do the hard work of raising a child alone. And most of them rise to the occasion and have amazing kids and wonderful lives."

"What are you saying?"

"I'm saying that either way you go, I think you'll do just fine, Miss Pike. I know you have a strong family system, and that goes a long way."

"I can't put this problem on my family."

She tilted her head. "Now, sweetie, do you really think that's how they'll feel? Or is it more likely they will be ecstatic and welcome this baby with open arms?"

She was right. Her family would always support her, no matter what. But could she do that to them?

"Why are you saying all of this?"

She sighed. "When I was seventeen years old, I became pregnant."

"Oh."

"In the end, I was forced to give my baby up. Times were different back then. The adoption was closed, so I've never been able to find my son. I know the heartbreak of giving a baby up."

"So why do you work for an adoption attorney?"

She smiled. "Things are very different now. Most adoptions are open, and I figured being inside of the system, I could make a difference."

"I'm sorry you had to give up your baby."

"Me too. But I believe he's out there living a great life, and that's all a mother can ask for, right?"

"Right."

"Well, I'd better get back," she said, putting the car back in gear and pulling into the driveway.

"Thanks, Karen."

"You're welcome, hon. You make the right decision for you and that baby, okay?"

"I'll try," Meg said, stepping out of the car. She waved as Karen drove out of sight. How was she ever going to get through this?

# CHAPTER 3

*J*ulie stood in front of the full length mirror on the back of her bedroom door. It had been a very long time since she'd felt quite so nervous about going on a date. Of course, she and Dawson had been on some very informal dates over the last couple of months, but meeting his friends from high school was another level.

"That dress looks beautiful on you!" Janine said as she walked into Julie's room. Janine was also going to the reunion with William.

Julie had always been a little envious of her sister's looks. She was petite with a full head of beautiful, curly hair, and sometimes Julie felt like a plain Jane standing next to her.

"Thanks. What are you wearing?"

"I'm wearing my blue dress with my silver strappy heels. Do you think that will look okay?"

Julie smiled. "I think you'll look beautiful, but then, you always do."

Janine elbowed her lightly. "Aw, shucks. Thanks, sis."

They continued getting ready, with Janine flitting in and out of the room, changing into her dress and putting on her heels. She stopped for a moment and stood behind Julie in the mirror.

"You okay?"

"What do you mean?"

"You seem a little... stressed? Or down?"

Julie sighed. "Well, events like this make me nervous. I haven't exactly dated in awhile, and meeting Dawson's lifelong friends is kind of like meeting his parents."

Janine smiled. "They're going to love you. Everyone does!"

"I wish I had your confidence," Julie said, laughing. "And then there's something else."

"What's that?"

Julie walked over and sat on the edge of her bed. "I'm a little worried about Meg."

"Worried? Why?"

"She's just acting strange. Like, she barely interacts with me, and she hasn't even visited the bookstore yet. I mean, I know she's a kid, and I know she's trying to readjust to life here, but I don't know. I guess I just expected her to be more excited about being back with her family."

Janine sat down beside her. "Oh, I think she's very excited to be here. Maybe she just misses her friends back in Europe."

"Maybe. I've just been waiting for her to come around, spend time with me, you know? Do you think she's mad at me for anything? Has she said anything to you?"

Janine paused for a moment longer than Julie would've expected and then smiled. "She hasn't said anything about you to me. She loves you, sis. I'm sure she'll come around soon. Just give her some time."

Julie nodded. "I'm sure you're right." She looked over at her phone sitting on the vanity. "Yikes, we'd better get a move on. The guys will be here in fifteen minutes!"

Colleen sat on the sand, her bare feet digging down into the softness. She pulled her thick cardigan tighter around her shoulders and stared at the ocean in front of her. The winds were milder tonight than normal, and she sucked in a long breath of the salty sea air. This place was intoxicating.

She'd been to plenty of beaches in California, but the low country areas of South Carolina were totally different. Mixtures of darkness and light, earthy smells and the glow of fireflies in the trees just behind her. Dawson had offered his private beach up to her anytime she needed a place to get away, and tonight was just such a night.

She was finding it hard to get back to regular life. She missed Peter in some ways, but never had any regrets about breaking up with him. More than anything, she missed having someone to talk to, someone who cared about how she was feeling. Actually, Peter had never been really good at those things anyway.

As she watched the faint light of a ship passing way out in the ocean, she thought about how different her life was now than just a few months ago. Gone were the swanky parties she'd attended with her law firm co-workers. Those had been replaced with a quick sandwich at the bistro and people watching on the square of her new town.

A few of her old co-workers kept in touch, usually just by a quick text, but those messages were getting fewer and farther between. Had they really been her friends? She laid back and stared up at the sky, now a solid black, and was amazed at how many stars she could see. There were no big streetlights to block her view. It was just her, the sound of the ocean and the flickering fireflies off in the distant thick tree-line.

She closed her eyes and took in a deep breath, like the ones her Aunt Janine did during her meditations. Before long, she felt herself drift off into that place between wakefulness and sleep. She hadn't meant to actually fall asleep, but the island wasn't a place she feared for her safety if she did. She could probably sleep all night, every night right in the middle of the beach and never have to worry.

"Ma'am, are you okay?" she suddenly heard a male voice say above her. All she could see was the outline of a male figure, the moon glowing behind the silhouette of his head.

She jumped to her feet, ready to employ those self defense skills she'd learned at her company retreat back in California. As she backed up a few steps, holding up her hands, she stared at the dark figure in front of her. How was she going to get past him and run fast enough to get away?

"I'm warning you, don't come any closer!"

The guy put up his hands and stood still. "I'm not trying to hurt you. I was just asking if you're okay."

He was young, probably around her age. She still couldn't see his face, the moon having been obscured by a passing cloud.

"This is a private beach. What are you doing here?"

"Oh, jeez. Sorry. I'm new around here, and a friend told me…"

"I don't care what anyone told you. You shouldn't…" she started to say. As the cloud passed, the moonlight shone down on the beach again and she realized she was talking to Tucker. The way too handsome new guy in town. Her secret crush. Her face turned red, but thank goodness he couldn't see that.

"I'm going to go…"

"No!"

"What?" He cocked his head to the side. "Wait. Didn't we meet the other day?"

She smiled. "Yes. I'm Colleen. I'm so sorry…"

He chuckled. "No need to be sorry. I shouldn't have walked up to you like that. It's just that I called out a couple of times, and you didn't answer."

"I must've fallen asleep. And, again, I apologize for trying to, you know, attack you."

Tucker smiled. "You had me a little scared, I have to admit. And I was in the Marines for a few years."

"Really? Wow. Well, thanks for your service."

"You're very welcome. So, can I ask why you're sleeping on a beach rather than in your own house?"

Colleen pointed at the sand before sitting down. Thankfully, he joined her. She felt like a giddy middle schooler, trying to keep her crush from switching to a different lunch table.

"I'm not actually homeless or anything. I live down the road there. My mother's... friend... owns that house over there. He lets me use this beach whenever I need some time to myself."

"And here I came over and ruined it."

"No, not at all," she said, struggling not to break her own face from smiling.

"So, what are you getting away from, exactly?"

Colleen sighed. "I think I'm taking my work home with me a little too much."

"You said you work as an attorney?"

"A starter attorney, I guess you'd say," she said with a laugh. "They sure don't pay me like a real one."

"And what kind of law do you practice?"

"Well, my firm is focused on a lot of domestic violence cases."

"Ah. I can see how that might be hard to handle."

"Yes. When I lived in California, we didn't do these kinds of cases, so it was easier to go home at night with a fairly clear head. But, hearing these stories all day... about women and children... and the circumstances... well, it's all a little much."

"I can only imagine. My job isn't nearly as stressful."

"What do you do?"

"I play with toys all day."

She stared at him, barely able to make out the blue color in his eyes. "Toys?"

"I'm a toy designer."

"That's a real job?" she said without thinking.

He chuckled. "I guess I'm pretty lucky. But, yes, it's a real job. I went to school for engineering, ended up in product design, and here I am. A start-up hired me right out of school, and we just relocated our offices here."

"Wow. So cool."

"It's a pretty laid back atmosphere. I mean, until we have a new launch. Then there's a lot of stress and contracts and deadlines."

"Maybe I'm in the wrong line of work. I can't imagine designing toys and playing with them all day. That sounds divine right about now."

"But your job makes such a difference. If you didn't do what you do, what options would those women and children have?"

She smiled. "Thanks for trying to make me feel better, but I basically push papers around and look at evidence. I don't do the real work."

"Don't sell yourself short. Everybody's job is important. Take mine for example. If I don't design a great educational toy for that kid who has a learning disability, who will? Or if I don't test a toy thoroughly, some kid could get hurt."

She looked back at the water, watching the moon

dance off of it. "To be honest, I wish I felt like my work mattered."

Colleen couldn't believe she was already baring her soul to this poor guy. All he did was stumble upon her on the beach. Now he was caught like a bear in a trap. She decided to give him an out.

"I know you must have something better to do than sit here and listen to a strange woman vent about her job," she said.

He smiled, big enough for her to see in the moonlight. "Are you kidding? I've been trying to work up the nerve to talk to you again for over a week."

Her heart started pounding. Was she dreaming? "What?"

"I don't want to interrupt your evening of sleeping on the beach, but would you want to have a cup of coffee with me, by chance?"

She smiled. "I would love that."

MEG STARED AT HER PHONE. Thank goodness she had the house to herself tonight. Aunt Janine and her mother were both gone to the reunion, and Colleen had wandered off again. Meg had no idea where she kept going at night, but she had her own problems to worry about.

Christian had texted her.

Her heart ached. She missed him. Even though she was only nineteen, she knew it had been real love. Their age difference hadn't mattered to either of them, and he'd treated her like a queen.

A tear rolled down her cheek as she imagined what he felt like when he realized she left in the middle of the night, hopping a plane back to America without a word. He had to be confused. She'd done it to protect him, to make sure he didn't lose his job. Even though he hadn't been her professor, if the university had found out a professor had impregnated a student, he might have lost his job.

She just couldn't take the chance.

After all, this was her fault. At least, that's how she saw it. On birth control since her teens for heavy periods, she'd always been good about taking her pills. Christian was the first guy she'd ever gotten that "close" with, and then one night they went further than she'd planned. Or hadn't planned. She'd let her prescription run out, never thinking they would cross that line before she had a chance to think it through.

But they did. He didn't push her into it. Honestly, it had been her idea. She got caught up in the romance of it all. An older man who adored her. The Paris skyline. The smell of baguettes everywhere she turned. Her brain had become mush, and she let her guard down. She made a split second decision that had turned into a lifetime commitment.

She hadn't told him she was pregnant, opting instead to pack her things and jump on an airplane without explanation. He had called and texted her for days, terrified something bad had happened to her. Finally, she sent him a text and told him they were through and that she had gone back home.

Christian had texted her back, begging and pleading, wanting to know what he did wrong. She could almost hear the tears in his words. But there was no way she was telling him the truth, that she was so irresponsible to have put herself in this position. In her mind, she had let so many people down lately. The only control she had was to make the best decision for her baby, no matter what it did to the rest of her life.

*Please, Meg. Call me. Text me. Anything. I'm so worried about you, my love. We can handle anything together. You can count on me.*

Ugh. Her heart broke as she stared at his words. She wanted to text him back, tell him the situation, ask him to come to America and be a family. But, she loved him too much to do that. She knew his career would be over, and she wasn't going back to Europe to raise her child, if she kept it. She wanted to be near her family if that happened. She needed them now more than ever, no matter what she decided.

So she turned her phone off. Answering him would only lead him on, and she felt a clean, swift break was the only way to go. Like pulling off a bandage stuck to a skinned knee. Better to just rip it off, feel the shocking pain and try to stand up again.

For tonight, the only thing that would help was a big tub of rocky road ice cream, a nice long cry and a warm bath.

JULIE HAD NEVER FELT SO out of place in her life. While her sister was having a blast, dancing around and meeting new people, she was stuck to Dawson's side like an appendage. She'd never been great at meeting new people, and with Dawson obviously being the best looking guy in the room, she felt judged. He was only three years younger, but right now she felt like he should just check her into the assisted living center down the road.

There were less than a hundred people at the reunion, which meant he'd obviously gone to a much smaller school than she had. But everyone knew everyone, and she knew three people in the whole place.

Dating in her forties wasn't something Julie had ever envisioned doing. She'd planned to stay married to Michael until they were old and gray, rocking grand babies on the front porch of their beach house. Things don't always work out how you think they will.

"You okay?" Dawson asked as they refilled their punch cups.

She smiled up at him. "Of course. This hotel is beautiful, and the shrimp and grits on the buffet are almost as good as Lucy's, but not quite."

"You're making small talk, and I've found that's never a good sign," he said, winking.

"I'm sorry. It's just that I have a bit of social anxiety, I guess."

He put his drink down and pulled her into a hug. "It's okay, Julie. I'm just grateful you came with me. I look a lot better with you on my arm."

She felt like melting into a puddle of goo right there on the floor.

"Dawson Lancaster?" a woman said from the other side of the table. She was drop dead gorgeous, like something out of a fashion magazine. Her long blond hair streamed down her back, her perfectly toned body adorned in a shimmery red dress with a slit up one side. Had she just come from the Miss America pageant or something?

"Tiffany?"

Uh oh. Tiffany? As in, the girl everyone had a crush on? That Tiffany? The one Dawson said would never come to the reunion?

Suddenly, Julie felt very inferior. She tried not to stare, but the woman looked like a supermodel. Was she aging in reverse? She tried to find a flaw, quickly, just to make herself feel better. Were her legs too long? Maybe her lips were a little too full? Nope. She was perfect, and Julie was a rumpled, stumpy old woman who needed to crawl under the nearest table and out the back door.

Or at least that's how she felt in the moment.

"Hi. I'm Tiffany. I don't think I remember you," she said, her Southern accent sounding like something out of a movie. She reached out her perfectly manicured hand, complete with the most expensive rings Julie had ever seen. Reluctantly, Julie shook her hand.

"Oh, no, I didn't go to your high school. I'm just here with Dawson." Here with Dawson? That made it sound like she was his homely cousin, just tagging along because she had nothing better to do.

"Well, nice to meet you, hon," she said in that sugary sweet way that Julie had always hated from the women she knew at the country club. Why did she feel so inferior? After all, she'd lived a pretty wealthy lifestyle herself. She was in the middle of the Atlanta social scene, her social calendar always booked up. But, the truth was she never felt like she fit in. The women were all phony, and the men were power hungry egomaniacs.

43

"I didn't expect to see you here," Dawson said, smiling down at her. Was he flirting? Surely not. But this was his high school crush, and those feelings often lingered. Julie hated how insecure she felt right now.

"I decided to come at the last minute. I couldn't pass up an opportunity to see everyone. I heard about Tania, and I'm just so sorry. She was a sweet girl," she said, rubbing Dawson's forearm. Julie wanted to slap it away.

"Julie, you've got to come do the electric slide with me!" Janine said, running up to her, breathless.

"No, thanks…" Julie tried to say before her sister yanked her arm and pulled her across the room. For a tiny person, Janine was strong as an ox. All those years of yoga, Julie supposed.

When they arrived on the dance floor, Janine immediately started dancing. Julie just stood there, staring across the room, expecting to see Tiffany lead Dawson out of the reunion at any moment.

"What are you looking at?" Janine said loudly, trying to talk over the music.

"My worst nightmare."

Janine looked over and finally noticed the beautiful blonde standing in front of Dawson. "Oh, her? Come on. She's nothing compared to you."

Julie turned and stared at her sister. "Have you been drinking?"

"Just a glass of wine. Why?"

"Look at her. She looks like God made her as an example for the rest of us to aspire to."

Janine stopped dancing, realizing her sister wasn't in a good place. She pulled her arm and led her outside, the cold air shocking both of their systems.

"What on Earth has gotten into you?" Janine asked quietly as other party goers passed by going to and from their cars.

"That woman was Dawson's high school crush."

"So?"

"She's stunning, Janine. I can't compete with that."

"Who says you have to? Dawson adores you, Julie. Just because this woman from twenty plus years ago came to the reunion doesn't mean he's interested in her."

"Oh, come on, Janine. Remember that huge crush you had on Dennis Compton?"

Janine smiled. "Ah, yes, Dennis. Denny. He was adorable. Had that fire engine red hair, and he let me cheat off of him in biology class."

"And if Denny showed up here tonight, you'd drop William like a hot potato!"

Janine laughed. "Um, no I wouldn't! Denny was a nerd. I've moved on, and so has Dawson, I'm sure. Besides, that woman may be married."

"Didn't stop my husband."

Janine sighed and put her hands on Julie's shoulders. "Is that what this is about? You don't trust men now because of what Michael did?"

"Maybe. I don't know."

"That's no way to live, sis. And you can't build something new with Dawson while punishing him for what Michael did."

"You're right. I'm being silly. Thanks," she said, hugging Janine.

"The song is almost over. Care to join me?"

"No, thanks. I'm going to stand out here and get a little air."

"Okay. Don't be too long."

Janine left her there on the sidewalk. She took a couple of deep breaths, trying to get her mind straight. As she turned around, through the window she saw Tiffany give Dawson a long hug. And then she handed him a piece of paper. Dawson quickly put it in his pocket as Tiffany walked away.

She couldn't go through this again. Maybe becoming a nun was a better option.

# CHAPTER 4

*D*awson looked at her as they walked up the steps to her front door. She'd tried to pretend she was okay for the rest of the night, but inside she just wanted to go home, put on her ugliest pajamas and eat whatever wasn't nailed down. Maybe she wasn't cut out for dating.

When she was young, the world was full of possible dates. Everyone was young and firm and had their whole lives ahead of them. Now, she felt like pickin's were slim, as her grandmother would say. Dawson was a rarity, the perfect combination of good looks and kindness, but every other woman who met him must have recognized the same thing she did. He was a catch.

"Are you okay? You've been kind of quiet."

"Just tired. I've been working so many days in a

row that I'm glad to have tomorrow off. I'm just going to clean the house, batch cook for next week and spend some time chilling out." Now, she was rambling.

"I hope I didn't do anything to upset you tonight?"

She smiled up at him. "Of course not." *Except when you exchanged numbers with that tart from your schoolboy crush days. That kind of sucked.*

"Good, because I had a great time with you," he said, leaning down and softly kissing her lips.

"Same here," she said, shakily, wishing she could muster the courage to ask him if he was leaving her house to go meet up with Tiffany the tart. "I'd better get inside."

"Right. Call you tomorrow?"

"Great."

He walked down the stairs, turned back one more time with a quizzical look on his face and then waved goodbye.

Julie opened the door and saw her sister and Meg sitting on the sofa. They looked like they were deep in conversation, which abruptly stopped when she walked inside. She leaned against the door and sighed.

"What's wrong?" Janine asked.

"Oh nothing. I'm just forty-three and dying on the vine," she said dramatically. She pulled off her coat and hung it on the rack by the door before sinking into the chair next to where they were sitting on the sofa.

Meg was wearing an oversized Paris sweatshirt, sweatpants and had a pillow in her lap, which was the perch for a large bowl of ice cream. She looked a bit like she'd been crying.

"You're not dying on the vine. Stop being ridiculous," Janine said rolling her eyes.

"She gave him her number. And he hugged her."

"So?"

"Wait. Who are we talking about?" Meg asked.

"Dawson's high school crush was at the reunion," Janine said, filling her in. "And your mother has it in her head that he's going to dump her and pursue Tiffany."

"Oh, Mom, come on. Dawson thinks you hung the moon. Even I can see that in my short time here. Besides, isn't this a little immature?"

Julie chuckled. "Give me a break. I haven't dated since I was around your age."

"I'm sure it was innocent, sis. Dawson's a nice guy. What was he supposed to do? Throw the paper back in her face?"

"Yes."

The three women all laughed at the absurdity of that image. Julie walked to the kitchen and grabbed a spoon. As she crossed back behind the sofa, she leaned over and took a big scoop of her daughter's ice cream before sitting back down. She kicked her heels off and put her feet on the coffee table.

"How'd you make it back here so fast?" Julie asked her sister.

"Dixie called William. Her toilet overflowed, so he had to go to her house to help her."

"Ah. So, Meg, when are you going to spend some time with your poor mother?"

Meg smiled. "Any time you want."

"Have you thought about looking for jobs here yet?"

Meg looked uncomfortable. "No. Not yet. I think I need a little more time to adjust. Is that okay?"

"Of course, honey. Just seems like you'd be bored around here. Maybe you could take some classes at the community college, just so you don't get behind."

"Mom, please. I just need a break."

"Sometimes breaks are hard to come back from. I'm just saying…"

"Mom! Just stop!" Meg suddenly jumped up and stormed out of the room, leaving her bowl of ice cream teetering on the pillow. Janine reached over and stopped it from tipping over.

"What on Earth?" Julie sat there, stunned, looking down the hallway where her daughter had gone.

"I think she's just tired," Janine said, filling her mouth with ice cream.

"Tired from what? Something is wrong. I know my daughter, and she's not herself. Maybe she needs to see a therapist?"

"Just give her time, sis."

Julie stared at her sister for a long moment. "Do you know something, Janine? And don't lie to me. I can always tell when you're lying."

Janine looked at her. "Julie…"

"I met the best guy!" Colleen announced as she opened the front door and held her arms in the air.

"What?" Julie said, turning around.

Colleen closed the door. "His name is Tucker, and he's the most adorable man to walk this planet." She grinned and did a little dance before shutting the door.

"Isn't this a little… soon?" Julie asked.

"I'm being a little dramatic, but seriously, this guy is amazing. I met him in town the other day, and tonight he scared me while I was taking a nap on Dawson's beach."

Janine's eyes opened wide. "You were taking a nap?"

"It was an accidental nap. Anyway, we talked and then went to have coffee. He designs toys for a living. Can you believe that? And he's so nice."

Julie smiled. "Well, I'm happy for you, sweetie."

"Thanks. Where's Meg?"

"In the bedroom. I upset her, but I'm not really

sure why. Maybe you could talk to her? See if she's okay?"

"Sure. I've got to go change and take a shower anyway."

Julie looked back at Janine, who was typing furiously on her phone. "I'm going to go meet William for coffee," she said, standing up. "Mind if I borrow your car?"

"Sure, but…"

She quickly kissed Julie on the head as she walked by. "We'll chat in the morning, sis. The coffee place isn't open that late."

Janine breezed out the front door, and Julie was more certain than ever that Janine was hiding something from her. And she didn't like it one bit.

COLLEEN WALKED into the bedroom to find Meg sitting on the bed, her legs pulled up to her chest with an oversized sweatshirt pulled down over them. Her eyes were puffy and red from crying, although she tried to hide that fact when she saw her sister walk into the room.

"Hey," Colleen said softly as she shut the door behind her. "Mom's worried about you."

"She just doesn't know when to stop pushing."

"Meg, what's going on?"

"What do you mean?" she said, wiping a stray tear from her eye and stretching her legs out as she pulled a bed pillow across her lap.

"What's with the pillow?"

"Huh?"

"You've being doing that a lot lately. Pulling a pillow across your lap. You've never done that before."

"It's cold."

Colleen eyed her carefully. "Sissy, I know you better than anyone, and something's up. Now, if you don't want to tell Mom, I get it. You can tell me anything. I won't tell a soul. I promise."

Meg looked at her for a long moment, obviously weighing her options. "I'm so ashamed," she said, her voice shaking as her eyes started overflowing yet again.

Colleen rushed over to her sister and sat down on the bed. "Oh my gosh, Meggy, what's wrong?"

"I'm... pregnant."

The room was completely silent for a moment as Colleen took in the information. "Pregnant?"

"Yes." Meg looked at her sister, as if she was trying to gauge her reaction. Colleen just sat there, staring straight ahead for a few moments. Meg sucked in a sharp breath and blew it out. "Say something."

"I'm just in shock right now, sis. I mean, I'm

going to be an aunt! And you're going to be a mommy!" Tears fell from Colleen's eyes as a smile spread across her face. She pulled the pillow away from Meg's belly and stared at the growing bump beneath her sweatshirt.

"Can you tell?" Meg asked, pointing at her stomach.

"Now I can. But that's because I know. I can't believe you're going to have a baby!"

"Shhh... I don't want Mom to hear you."

"Meg, you have to tell Mom soon. It's getting a little more obvious. Why haven't you told her? She's worried."

Meg stood up and walked to the mirror, turning sideways to survey her belly. "Because I don't want her to be disappointed in me, Colleen. Who wants to tell their mother that they got knocked up in France and need help?"

Colleen stood behind her sister in the mirror. "We'll do this together. Let's go out there and tell her now. After all, we need time to get a nursery ready. Oh, I am so excited! I can't wait to do all the baby clothes shopping. Have you seen what they have at that baby boutique on the square? Adorable! Absolutely adorable..."

"Colleen! Stop!" Meg held up her hand.

"What's wrong?"

"I don't know how to say this... I've met with an adoption attorney."

"What? You have to be kidding me, Meg. Please don't tell me you're planning to give my niece or nephew away."

Meg sat down on the edge of the bed. "I haven't made up my mind."

"But, why? You have family. We're here for you and the baby. Adoption is for people who..."

"People who what?"

Colleen sat down. "I don't know. People who don't have support? People who don't want to raise a child?"

"Look, I don't need this extra pressure, okay? I've already heard it from Aunt Janine."

"Aunt Janine knows? Are you insane? You told her and not Mom? She's going to freak out, and they're going to stop speaking all over again!"

"Hold your voice down! I didn't tell her. She overheard me making my OBGYN appointment and then confronted me. I swore her to secrecy."

"Meg, this whole thing is getting out of hand. You have to tell Mom."

"Just give me another week, okay? I need to make a decision about this adoption, and I can't do that with everyone pressuring me, especially Mom."

"Meg..."

"Please, Colleen. One more week."

Colleen sat silently. "Fine. A week."

"Thanks. I need to get some sleep," Meg said, crawling back up toward her pillow. Colleen pulled the covers up around her neck and kissed her forehead, something she'd done a lot as they were growing up. They weren't far apart in age, but Colleen had always thought of Meg as her baby.

"Goodnight, Meggy."

As she watched her sister drift off to sleep, albeit a restless one, Colleen wondered what this news was going to do to their mother. And what was her mother going to do if she found out Janine had known the whole time?

JULIE PICKED up the big box of books and set it on the counter. Business was starting to pick up as the colder weather was getting behind them, and more tourists were starting to descend on the town.

"I think we should set up a whole display of those new self-help books. People love those things," Dixie said, chuckling. "Personally, I don't think I could improve myself any more than the way God made me, but I don't mind selling books to people who think they need all that rubbish advice."

"Well, I don't think that's the best way for us to

sell them," Julie said, giggling. "Maybe calling them rubbish isn't the best marketing terminology."

Dixie waved her hand at Julie and started clearing off a bookshelf to make way for the new inventory. "I meant to ask you, how did the reunion go with Dawson the other night?"

"It was nice."

"That sure doesn't sound exciting," Dixie said, turning around and looking at her.

Julie sighed. "I don't know. I think I'm overreacting. Actually, my own nineteen-year-old daughter said I was being immature, if that tells you anything. "

"Immature about what?"

"Well, Dawson told me about how he had this huge crush on a girl in high school. He said she was basically a Barbie doll, and her name was Tiffany. And wouldn't you know it? Tiffany shows up at the reunion, and she's all over Dawson. Rubbing his arm, giving him a hug."

"Oh, sweetie, you don't have to worry about Dawson. He's as loyal as the day is long."

Julie pulled some books out of the box and handed them to Dixie. "I know he's loyal. I just don't want him to be tied down to me if he'd rather date that blonde supermodel."

Dixie turned around and and cocked her head. "Well, what do you think you are? Chopped liver?"

"I felt that way standing next to her."

"Darlin', Dawson really likes you. He's not the type of guy to chase some skirt around just because she's cute."

Julie sat down in the chair and put her head in her hands. "I don't know why I'm acting like this. I'm a grown woman, for goodness sakes! I guess after what happened with Michael… and the fact that I haven't dated since I was a teenager myself…"

Dixie sat down across from her and held her hands. "Sugar, it will all work out. Just don't make any silly decisions in the heat of the moment. Trust Dawson. He's a good man."

"You're right. In fact, you're always right, and it's quite annoying."

Dixie let out a loud laugh. "I sure wish my Johnny was here so you could tell him how I'm always right. He never would admit it while he was alive!"

The two women continued stocking the shelves, chatting about this and that. Julie was surprised when she looked up and saw her daughter, Meg, standing outside the bookstore.

She ran to the door and opened it, the loud bell echoing in the empty bookstore. "Meg! I'm so glad you decided to come see our bookstore."

Meg smiled, looking almost uncomfortable. "I figured it was about time. I wanted to check out the town, so I had Aunt Janine and William drop me off while they go do some work at the studio."

"Well, I'm glad you're here. Come on in. I want you to meet Dixie, my friend and business partner."

She brought Megan into the bookstore and gave her the grand tour. Dixie gave her a hug, as she did any new person she met. But there was a strange look on Dixie's face when she pulled back from hugging Meg. Julie couldn't put her finger on it, but some communication happened between Meg and Dixie that wasn't put into words.

"So, what do you think?"

"It's adorable. There was a little bookstore on the outskirts of Paris that I used to love to go to with…" Meg stopped short and then looked down at her feet. It was obvious to Julie that she was missing her boyfriend back in Europe, and she couldn't understand why Meg had chosen to leave the country and have no contact with him. She worried that he had done something bad to her, but she tried not to think about it. She wanted to give Meg the space to tell her whatever had happened when she was ready.

"Well, I'd better get going. I promised Colleen that I would meet up with her for lunch."

Julie's eyebrows knitted together in confusion. "Oh. Y'all are having lunch? I would've loved to have joined you."

"I know. We didn't think you'd want to because

we're just going to be talking about Colleen's new love interest. You know, sister stuff."

There was a long awkward pause. "Right. Well, I have so much to do here anyway. Maybe we can do it another time."

"Great. See you at home later," Meg said, making her way out of the store quickly. As she disappeared down the sidewalk, Julie turned back to Dixie.

"Something is definitely off with her."

"Maybe you should just sit down and have a heart to heart talk with her, hon. I think she might be going through a rough patch."

Julie cocked her head. "Why do you say that?"

"Oh, just old woman intuition, I suppose."

JANINE ROLLED out her yoga mat and stretched her arms high above her head. She needed this practice today. Keeping Meg's secret was wearing on her in ways she couldn't describe. She hated keeping things from her sister, and this was the biggest kind of secret.

"You'll have to teach me how to do that," William said as he walked around the corner.

"Oh yeah?"

"I can't even touch my toes, I'm so stiff. How did I snag myself a real life yogi with my inflexible body?"

She laughed. "Good question. Let's not pull at that string."

"So, I was going over your budget, like you asked. I have some questions."

"Okay, shoot," she said, as she fell forward and put her hands on the ground, her head hanging between her legs.

"This line item for grief, what does that mean?"

She stood back up and pulled her foot up in the air and to the side, struggling to maintain her balance as she looked at him. "I want to do some free classes for people in the local grief counseling groups. They were a big help to me, so I want to give back."

"Oh. Gotcha. What about this free workshop in June?"

"That's for the stay at home and single mothers. I know they can't always afford regular yoga classes, but it's so important for mental health." She leaned forward again and went into downward facing dog pose.

"And the mommy and me classes. Don't you think the rate for those is a little low?"

She popped back up and looked at him. "They're new mommies, William. Do you think they have unlimited income for yoga classes?"

He smiled slightly. "Do you?"

"Do I what?"

"Have unlimited income?"

"No…"

"Janine, you asked me to help you with this place, to make sure you were successful. And I have to say…"

"What?"

"Now, don't take this the wrong way, but you're not the best business person I've ever met."

She put her hands on her hips and glared at him. "That was rude! And I never claimed to be a business person. I'm a yoga teacher!"

"When you decided to open this place, you became a business person too, Janine. And right now, if you keep making plans like this, this place will go under in a matter of weeks."

She was fuming now. "As my boyfriend, aren't you supposed to support me no matter what?"

"I'm trying to support you, honey… by telling you the truth. If you give away free classes and discounts, you won't be able to pay your bills, much less yourself."

"I teach yoga to help people." She walked over to the desk and took a sip of water.

"You can't be so…"

"So what?"

"Naive. New Age. Head in the clouds."

"Get out!"

"Excuse me?"

She pointed toward the door. "Get out, Will! If you think those things of me, then we obviously aren't meant to be!"

He walked toward her. "Come on now, Janine. You're just upset…"

"Don't patronize me! Get out! Right now!"

William looked at her for a moment before quietly turning and walking out the door, placing the notepad he had in his hand on the desk as he walked by. She watched him walk down the sidewalk and out of sight before the first tears started to fall.

# CHAPTER 5

"So, where did you grow up?" Colleen asked Tucker as they sat together at lunch. This had been their routine for the last week, meeting for lunch at the bistro down the road from both of their offices. A couple of times, he'd shown her samples of toys he was testing. Other times, he'd shown her drawings on his iPad of new toys he was working on. She found the whole thing intriguing.

"Right outside of Nashville, actually."

"And you didn't become a country music star? Even with a name like Tucker?"

He smiled. "I'll have you know that I wanted to be a country music singing sensation. I wanted to be on the Grand Old Opry and win a music award."

"Well, what happened?"

"Turns out I can't carry a tune in a bucket."

Colleen laughed. "That makes two of us. When I was in middle school, my horribly mean theatre teacher made me take a singing part in Oklahoma. I just remember standing there, on stage in front of family and classmates, and freezing. My mouth literally wouldn't move. The only sound that came out was some kind of croaking noise that sounded like I'd swallowed a frog!"

"You poor thing," he said, taking a bite of his chicken salad sandwich.

"Yes, I'm still very traumatized by it."

"So, do you have siblings?"

"Just one. A sister. Her name is Meg, and she's nineteen."

"I have two brothers, both older, both married with kids. Todd lives in Colorado and runs a tech firm. Mark lives in Montana and has a cattle ranch, of all things."

"And you play with toys?"

"Living the dream."

"I think you are. When you have kids one day, you'll be the coolest father out there." As soon as she said it, she felt like she'd put her foot in her mouth.

"Thanks. I hope to be a father one day."

"Oh yeah? Do you want a big family?"

"I'd like to have three kids, I think. Of course, my

wife would have to agree to that. I don't think I should get the deciding vote on that one."

"Good answer," she said, smiling as she sipped on her sweet tea. She found herself enjoying his company so much more than she expected. He was easygoing, and she just felt comfortable sitting with him.

"What about you? Are kids in your future?"

"I hope so. I mean, I'm still young. I'll be twenty-two in a few months, but I definitely want to have kids one day. I thought I was getting closer to that life recently…" Foot in mouth all over again.

"Really? Why is that?"

She sighed. "I recently broke off an engagement."

Tucker seemed surprised. "I'm sorry to hear that."

"Don't be. It was for the best. We were not a good match."

"Well, I have to say I'm glad because otherwise we wouldn't have met, right?"

"Right," she said, struggling to contain her smile.

"And I really enjoy your company, Colleen."

"I enjoy yours too."

"Good. So, would you like to… um… go on an actual date sometime?"

She grinned. "I thought you'd never ask."

DIXIE STOOD at the front register, watching people pass by on the street outside the shop. She loved to people watch. Mainly, she liked to make up stories about them as they walked by.

She was surprised to see Julie's daughter, Meg, walk through the door.

"Well, hello again, young lady!" Dixie said with a smile.

"Hi."

"Your Mom isn't working today, hon. She had a dental appointment over in Charleston."

Meg smiled. "Yes, I know. I just thought I'd come browse around a bit, if you don't mind?"

"Of course. Can I get you a cup of coffee? We have a new French roast that's heavenly."

Meg paused for a moment. "No, thanks. I've been trying to cut back on coffee."

Dixie eyed her carefully. "I understand. Well, make yourself at home, sweetie. I'm going to do a little cleaning behind this register."

"Thanks."

Meg walked toward the back of the store, looking at Dixie one more time before disappearing behind a bookshelf. If she didn't know the girl, she might have thought she was a shoplifter. She was definitely hiding something, and Dixie felt certain she knew what it was.

It wasn't in Dixie's nature to hold her tongue, and

she immediately knew this time wasn't going to be any different. She quietly walked to the back of the store and could see Meg looking at the pregnancy books. Surely, a young girl like herself could find all sorts of information on the Internet, but she seemed engrossed in whatever pregnancy book she was holding.

Dixie felt a pang go through her chest. She remembered what that felt like. Back in her teenage years, she'd found herself pregnant too. It was the most tumultuous, scary time of her life. A few weeks in, she'd lost that baby, something she'd never really gotten over to this day.

"Honey?"

Meg turned around quickly, trying to hide the book behind her back. "Oh. You scared me," she said, her voice shaking.

"It's okay. I won't tell anyone."

"Tell anyone what?"

"That you're pregnant."

Meg's eyes opened wide, and she laughed nervously. "What in the world would make you think that?"

Dixie leaned against a bookshelf, one of the things she often did to stabilize herself after her Parkinson's diagnosis. "Well, darlin', when I gave you that hug a few days ago, I felt a baby bump as clear as day."

"I've just put on some weight recently. All those baguettes in France, I guess," she said, giggling nervously.

"Sweetie, it's time to admit the truth, isn't it?"

Meg hung her head. "Oh no... Did you say something to my mother?"

"No, of course not. That's not my business, hon. But, your momma is sure worried about you, and I think you need to be honest with her. A girl needs her mother when she's pregnant."

Meg put the book back on the shelf and sighed. "I do need her. I hate lying to her."

"Then why're you doing it?"

She shrugged her shoulders. "I just can't take the thought of my mother being disappointed in me like that. Do you know how proud she was to tell everyone that I had straight A's in high school? And that I got into a university in Europe with a full ride scholarship? She was just beaming. And now I'm supposed to tell her that I'm knocked up, unmarried and no longer in school?"

Dixie smiled. "Mommas love their babies, no matter what. Life doesn't always take a straight course, sweetie. Your Mom knows that. She'll love you and be proud of you no matter what. Now, I'm not saying she won't be shocked as heck, but she'll get over that."

"I'm actually planning on telling her this week-end. We have a family dinner planned, so I don't want to ruin it. But the next morning, I'm going to do it. I can't wait anymore. Besides, my Aunt Janine and my sister know now, so it's only a matter of time before Mom finds out."

"Wait. They know and your Mom doesn't? Oh, hon, that's not good."

"I know. I didn't intend for that to happen."

Dixie walked closer and put her hands on Meg's shoulders. "You're going to be a momma soon. Time to deal with the hard stuff head on, okay? Tell your mother."

Meg smiled as a tear escaped her eye. "I will. I promise."

Dixie took the book off the shelf and handed it to her. "Here. This is my gift to you."

"Oh, I couldn't…"

"Take it. Really."

Meg took it and slipped it in her tote bag. "Thank you."

"You're welcome. And congratulations, little momma."

JULIE PRESSED down on the potato masher with all her force, and probably more than was needed for potatoes.

"Why are you so angry today? We're having a nice family dinner, but you're acting like a rabid wolverine right now," Janine said, taking the masher out of her hands.

"I'm not angry," Julie said, turning her attention to the biscuit dough. She punched and pulled at it, rolling it out on the countertop.

"Julie, come on. What's up?"

She stopped and sighed. "I guess it's this whole thing with Dawson. I've tried to pretend I didn't see him and Tiffany exchanging numbers, but I just can't."

"Why don't you just ask him about it?"

"Seriously? And you think he'd tell me the truth? Men always hide whatever they need to."

"Julie, this is Dawson we're talking about. Have you forgotten what a great guy he is?"

She hung her head. "Maybe I have. Of course, I haven't seen him much this week. Every time I invite him to get together, he tells me he's just really busy working right now. We live on an island. How busy could he be?"

"Is he coming today?"

"Who knows? I invited him, and he said he'd try to stop by."

"What's for dinner?" Colleen asked as she breezed into the kitchen. Ever since she met Tucker, she'd been all smiles, constantly in a good mood.

Julie was excited to meet him soon, although Colleen wasn't quite ready to bring him to Sunday dinner. With her girls home, she wanted to create a new tradition, and this meal was just the way to do that.

"Well, we're having grilled lemon chicken, mashed potatoes, biscuits and a cherry cobbler for dessert," Julie said, planting a smile on her face. "Where's Meg?"

"I think she's freshening up. She'll be out here in a minute."

"How much freshening up does a nineteen-year-old need to do?" Julie said with a laugh. "I'd give anything to be that age again."

"Tell me about it," Janine said.

"Hello?" Dawson said as he walked in the front door. He was dressed nicely, in his best jeans and a white button up shirt.

Julie smiled slightly. "Hey. Glad you could make it."

"Of course. Wouldn't miss it. Here, I brought some of Lucy's famous sweet tea." He handed her a jug, and she immediately felt bad. There was no way Dawson would hide something from her, especially not knowing her history. She was just being ridiculous. As she looked up at him, her heart melted a bit.

"Thanks. I love Lucy's tea."

Dawson gave her a quick kiss on top of her head,

something he did a lot, and waved at Janine and Colleen. "Can I do anything?"

"Nope. We've got it covered. Make yourself at home," she said, pointing at the sofa. The TV already had some game on, and she was sure Dawson would have no trouble amusing himself.

"Well, don't you look cute," Julie said as Meg walked into the living room. She was wearing an oversized pink sweater and a pair of jeans. "But I think that sweater's a bit big on you, sweetie. You're such a tiny thing, like your Aunt Janine. Show off that young figure while you can!"

Meg sucked in a sharp breath. "It's just the style, Mom," she said, with that teenager attitude that most parents recognized well.

"It's adorable, honey. I wasn't trying to pick a fight…" Julie started to say, but Meg just rolled her eyes and walked into the living room, plopping down into the chair and closing her eyes. "Is she okay?" Julie asked, looking at Colleen for some kind of help.

"She's just hormonal," Colleen said.

"Oh. I see. Should I get her some pain medication?"

"No!" Colleen and Janine said a the same time. Julie looked at them quizzically.

"What's wrong with you two?"

Janine laughed. "Oh, we probably saw the same

news report about those medications. They can cause an increased heart attack and stroke risk. Much better to just take an epsom salt bath and use a heating pad."

Julie stared between them for a moment. "Okay then…"

"Hello, hello!" Dixie called as she walked in the house. Julie loved the ease with which her friends came into her home. They were all like family now. William followed behind his mother, holding a covered dish. Dixie never showed up without something.

"Glad you could come," Julie said, hugging Dixie and then William. She noticed Janine glaring at him and assumed they were still in a spat about his business advice and her inability to listen. She decided to stay out of it because she could honestly see both sides of the situation.

"I brought my mother's famous potato salad. She was the best cook I've ever known. Wait until you try it!" Dixie said.

Julie took the bowl from William. "I'll be looking forward to that then. Have a seat and relax. We'll be ready to eat shortly."

For the next twenty minutes, Julie, Janine and Colleen worked in the kitchen, making sure everything was ready. Dawson, not able to stop himself from helping, took food from the kitchen and put it on the table. Meg set the table, still not looking at her mother or speaking to anyone. Julie was growing more and more worried by the moment. It sure didn't seem like she was just hormonal. After all, she had raised her daughter during those dreaded high school years, and she knew what her hormone surges looked like. This wasn't it.

They sat down at the table and said grace, something Julie loved to do. It felt like a real family, problems and all.

"So, did you get a call from Mom today too?" Janine asked Julie.

"No, why?"

"She and Buddy are taking a cruise to the Bahamas, and she sent me some pictures of her cruise wear. All I can say is God bless those poor Bahamian people. I hope they're color blind."

Everyone laughed, even Meg. Julie tried not to stare at her, but she wanted to make everything okay. She just wanted her daughters to be happy.

As with most of Julie's dinners, there was suddenly a knock at the door, interrupting the lively conversation that was going on around the table. She walked over and answered the door, but didn't recognize the man standing there.

"Can I help you?"

"Yes, please. I'm looking for Meg..." he leaned around and saw Meg looking at the door, her eyes wide. "Meg, my darling!" Without warning, he moved past Julie and into the house.

"Christian…" she said softly. She didn't get up. Instead, she just kept staring at him.

"You're Christian? From France?" Julie asked. He turned back to her.

"Yes, madame. I'm so sorry to interrupt your meal, but I've been trying to reach Meg for weeks now. I had to know she was okay."

"Christian, you shouldn't have come here."

The room was silent, everyone looking at the man with the thick French accent like he'd just landed from Mars.

"Maybe we could take a walk?" he asked.

"No, Christian. Please go. You see that I'm okay." Meg looked down at her hands in her lap, and Julie felt a surge of motherly anger. This guy must have hurt her. Maybe he was abusive.

"You need to leave. My daughter obviously doesn't want you here," Julie said, touching his arm.

Dawson and William both stood up.

"Meg, please."

She still didn't look up.

"Okay, fella, it's time for you to head back to the Eiffel Tower," Dawson said, walking around the table.

"It's alright. I will leave. But I need to just ask Meg one question. Please. And then I will go."

Dawson stopped and crossed his arms.

Christian reached into his pocket and pulled out a plastic bag. He held it up toward Meg. "I need to know why I found this positive pregnancy test in your bathroom waste bin?"

hy did Julie's dinner parties always end up with some unexpected person showing up at her door and creating chaos?

The silence in the room was deafening as Christian stood there, like some European statue, holding what appeared to be a positive pregnancy test in the air.

"Meg?" Julie finally said softly. Her daughter continued staring down at her hands. "Say something, honey. Tell him he's made a mistake."

When she looked up, tears streaming down her face, Julie had her answer. How hadn't she noticed that her daughter was pregnant? Had she been so wrapped up in her petty day to day life worries that she didn't even realize her daughter was struggling?

"I'm so sorry, Mom..." she said, sobbing uncontrollably.

"We should go," Dixie said to the others, waving for everybody to get up.

"No, it's okay," Meg said, slowly standing up. "Everybody might as well hear what an irresponsible, immature person I am." She wiped her eyes and finally looked at Christian. He was standing there, the bag in his hand by his side, his eyes wide.

"Meg, why didn't you tell me? Why did you just leave without a word? I was broken hearted."

"I know, and I'm so sorry. I didn't want to risk you losing your job. You've worked your whole life for that."

Julie continued standing by the front door, her body frozen. She didn't know what to say or do. Her daughter, her baby, was pregnant. How could that be?

"Mom? Are you okay?"

"Yeah, I'm just..." And that was the last thing Julie remembered until she saw Dawson's face hovering over her.

"Oh, thank God. She's coming to," he said.

Julie's eyes felt glazed over as she looked up to see the ceiling fan above her. "What happened?"

"You fainted, hon," Dixie said.

"Wow. I haven't had that happen in years," Julie said, trying to sit up.

"Easy does it," Dawson said, slowly helping her up to a seated position. "No sudden movements."

"I'm fine. Meg, I'm so sorry," she said, looking over at her daughter, who was sitting on the floor beside her.

"No, I'm sorry, Mom. I didn't want to disappoint you. That's why I didn't tell you."

Julie felt awful that she fainted in the middle of her daughter's worst life moment. She wasn't one to be dramatic or try to take attention away from her kids. They were her world. Her heart ached when she realized just how little she knew about her daughter. She'd been so wrapped up in her worries about Dawson that she hadn't even noticed her daughter's obvious baby bump?

"Now, we really are all going to go and give you some time to talk. Call me if you need anything, Julie," Dixie said, ushering William and Dawson to the door.

"I'm going to go too, Mom. Me and Aunt Janine are going to just take a walk and give you some time."

Julie nodded as she watched everyone walk out of the room, except for Christian, who continued standing there like he didn't know exactly what to do.

"Christian, why don't you sit down," Julie said,

pointing at a chair next to where they were sitting on the floor.

She couldn't remember a time in her life when she felt more awkward. Here was a guy that she didn't know, but her daughter was carrying his baby. Suddenly, their age difference popped into her head and made her even more uneasy. Her daughter was still just a baby herself, even though she was turning twenty in just a few weeks. She wasn't ready to be a mom, to be hit with all of the emotions that motherhood brought.

"Meg, I don't understand why you ran away," Christian finally said.

"I told you. I love you, and I didn't want you to lose everything you'd built. Not only would you get into all kinds of trouble, if not fired, for dating a student at the University, but having a baby right now would have thrown off your career path."

He shook his head, a stray tear rolling down his face. "It's our baby."

"I understand that. I was just trying to keep you from having to make impossible decisions. Look, Christian, I know you're a good man. I know you would've done the right thing, but I didn't want you to feel obligated to me. This was *my* mistake."

"Wait just a minute!" Julie said, holding up her hand. "I'm sorry, but this was not all your fault, Meg. This man is much more experienced than you are, and this sure didn't happen without his involve-ment," she said, very uncomfortable talking about her daughter's sex life.

"Mom, you know I've been on birth control for my cycles all these years. I ran out, and I just got lazy. And then I decided to go further than I planned..."

"Please, Meg. There's only so much I can take in one day. I don't need to know the details."

"Your mother is right, Meg. This isn't your fault. I was there too."

"But you didn't know I wasn't taking my pills. That was all on me."

"Look, both of you made mistakes. The baby is the most important issue now. Have you even been getting prenatal care?"

Meg nodded. "Of course, I have. I'm not stupid."

"How many weeks along are you?"

"I'm about halfway through my pregnancy."

Julie's eyes widened. "You've been keeping this a secret for half of your pregnancy? I can't believe you didn't tell me. I'm your mother."

She wanted to dissolve into a puddle of tears. All of these years, she thought she was being a great mom to her girls. She wanted to be a wonderful example of a woman, wife and mother. And now her daughter was pregnant and didn't even tell her. It made her feel like the world's biggest failure as a parent.

"I just didn't want you to be disappointed in me. And I know you are."

Julie put her arm around her daughter, pulling her head to her shoulder. "I'm your mother. I may not always like what you girls do, but I love you and I will always support you. No, this isn't what I expected. But this is my grandchild, and I can't wait to meet him or her."

Meg sat up and looked at her. "Mom…"

"And this is my child. Don't you think I should get a say so in what goes on?" Christian asked, a hint of irritation in his voice. "I mean, I can't believe you ran away and took my baby with you. That's not fair, Meg."

Meg stood up, running her fingers through her hair in frustration. "I've met with an adoption attorney."

Julie and Christian both looked shocked. Julie decided to stay on the floor, not wanting to risk passing out again. This was all too much to take.

"You were going to give our baby away without even talking to me?" Christian said, standing up to face her. "This is *our* child!"

"I know that! Don't you think I've thought about every possible scenario? It's all I think about! I don't know what I want to do, but I want to be ready. I'm nineteen years old. I can't do this alone, and it's not fair to a baby!"

"Who says you have to do this alone? I was there! I would've never left you or the baby!" Christian said.

"I know you wouldn't. But I'm not sure *I'm* ready," she said.

Julie's heart clenched in her chest. The thought of losing her first grandchild made her want to cry, but she held it together. She had to realize that Meg was an adult now, capable and able to make her own decisions. And this was a life-changing decision, for her and the baby. More than anything, she wanted to scoop her daughter up in her arms and make all of her problems go away. She wanted to offer to adopt the baby herself.

Slowly, Julie stood up and faced her daughter. "You don't have to make any decisions right now. I'm just glad that I know. I'm not disappointed in you, Meg. I love you, and I want to help you through this in whatever way you need me."

She said the words, but she only partially meant them. She was a bit disappointed that her daughter had squandered her educational opportunities in Europe in favor of shacking up with an older man and getting pregnant. But she surely wasn't going to say that. And she felt guilty for even feeling it.

She also wasn't being quite honest about helping

her in whatever way she could. She wanted to scream at the top of her lungs that she didn't want Meg to give away her grandchild. But that wasn't her decision to make. She felt very selfish thinking those things, but as long as she didn't say them out loud, they were her's to feel bad about.

"Meg, I think we need to talk more about this." Christian looked just as devastated as Julie felt inside. "Can we go somewhere?"

"Christian, I'm not ready right now. All of this has been such a shock, you showing up here without warning. I think I just need to go lay down for a while."

He nodded and looked at his feet. "I'm going to go over that bridge and get a hotel room. I'm not leaving until we settle this. I love you, and that hasn't changed. Please don't make decisions without me. That's my baby too." Without another word, he turned and walked out the front door, getting into a rental car and driving away.

Julie looked at Meg. She looked like she had the whole world weighing on her shoulders. "You go get in the bed. I'm going to make you a nice cup of tea. If you're hungry, we have plenty of food," Julie said, laughing sadly.

"I'm not very hungry. But tea sounds nice."

Meg started walking toward her bedroom. "We will get through this," Julie said.

Meg turned around and looked at her mother. "I know, but my life will never be the same no matter what choice I make. And that terrifies me."

As THE DAYS PASSED, Julie finally came to the realization that her daughter actually was pregnant and they were going to have to figure out what to do. Meg had not wanted to talk more about it for the last few days, opting instead to stay in her room most of the time. Julie was getting worried about her mental health on top of everything else.

Christian had stayed in town, dropping by the house a couple of times, hoping that Meg would talk to him. Every time, she instructed her mother to send him away. She just wasn't emotionally ready to deal with it.

As Julie sat across from Dixie, she hoped for some kind of motherly advice that would pull her family out of the mess they were in. Dixie always seemed to know what to say and what to do. Right now, she needed someone to take the reins. Even though she was a forty something-year-old mother, she felt like she wasn't equipped to deal with everything going on around her. And the last person she could call for advice was her own mother, the most critical person on the planet.

"I'm just so worried about her. She said that she's getting regular prenatal care, but I don't know who she has been seeing since she's been here."

"You have to trust her, Julie. She's going through a lot right now. Just give her a few days to get used to the idea that you know. Her biggest fear was that you were going to be disappointed in her."

"I know, and I don't know where she got that from. I've always been so encouraging to my daughters."

Dixie smiled and reached across the table, putting her hand on top of Julie's. "Our kids want to impress us. They want to make us smile, make us proud. Even when they don't want to admit it. And to have to come back home pregnant, having lost her opportunity at the University, I'm sure she felt like there would be no way around you being disappointed in her."

"I mean, I guess a part of me is a little disappointed. Not in her, but the situation. This just wasn't what I envisioned for my daughter."

"Well, we don't always get to choose how our kids turn out. We can only love them and support them, but in the end they have to take responsibility for their life choices."

"I know. And at least I know that she did come by the bookstore the other day to get that pregnancy book. That made me feel better about her state of mind."

Dixie looked at her, cocking her head slightly to the side. "You're not mad at me then?"

"Mad at you? Why would I be mad?"

"I guess I just thought that you would be upset that I knew Meg was pregnant before you did."

Julie stared at her, her mouth hanging open. "What do you mean?"

Dixie's face changed to one of surprise. "Oh. I thought you knew…"

"You thought I knew what?"

Dixie sighed and looked down at her hands. "Boy, I really stuck my foot in my mouth this time."

"Dixie, what are you talking about?"

"When I gave Meg a hug that first day, I felt her little pregnant belly. So, she came by the shop the other day to look at some books. Being the sneaky old woman that I am, I went to see what she was looking at and it was the pregnancy books. So, I told her I knew she was pregnant. She just fell apart."

"You knew and you didn't tell me? How could you do that?" Julie felt a rage well up inside of her. She knew Dixie probably meant no harm by it, but this was *her* daughter. She couldn't believe Dixie wouldn't have told her what she knew so that she could have helped her sooner.

"Honey, I didn't do it to hurt you. It's just such a

big secret, and I encouraged her to tell you. I just didn't feel it was my place."

"You're a stranger to her, and she felt more comfortable talking to you about it?"

"No, darlin', I'm just a good guesser. She wasn't going to tell me diddly squat. I gave her that book, in a way hoping you'd find it."

Julie sighed. "I'm sorry. I didn't mean to get so upset with you. It's just that I don't understand why my daughter would tell anyone other than her own mother."

"Again, to be fair, she didn't tell me. I guessed."

Julie smiled sadly. "And that's what upsets me even more. I've hugged my daughter several times since she came home, and I didn't notice. I've been so wrapped up in my own stupid problems that I haven't been paying enough attention to her."

"Now, don't beat yourself up. You had no reason to believe that your daughter came home with a baby on board."

"Yes, but I've been so focused on working, helping Dawson renovate his house, writing my book…"

"As you should be! Look, I know you love your kids, but they are adults now. All you can do is be there for them. You can't run their lives. You have to have your own life too. You deserve it."

"I know. It's just so hard to balance all of this.

And Michael doesn't even know. Meg won't let me tell him, and I just don't feel right about that. But she said she doesn't need any more pressure."

"I get that. It would be hard for her to make a decision about this with everybody giving their input. But, surely she'll want to tell her father pretty soon."

"I hope so."

As they continued chatting and eating lunch, Julie looked up and noticed Dawson down the road on the other side of the sidewalk. She thought about standing up and waving her hand, to invite him over to have lunch with them. But before she could do that, she saw Tiffany.

She was walking out of a restaurant behind him, the two of them laughing and talking. Julie's guts churned. As much as she didn't want to be worried about her own romantic life right now, she couldn't help but feel jealousy. After all, Dawson had told her he was working today, and yet here he was having lunch with his high school crush.

She thought about saying something to Dixie, but she didn't. After all, Dawson was like a son to Dixie. And even though she was close to her also, she couldn't compete with the long history the two of them had. So, she pushed her feelings down by taking another big bite of her sandwich and trying to look in the other direction.

By the time she looked up again, they were gone. Probably going to have a romantic walk on the beach or ride a bicycle built for two. She wanted to throw up.

"Are you okay?" Dixie asked, turning around to see what Julie was looking at.

"Oh, yeah. I just saw this sickening couple down the road."

Dixie laughed. "Don't ya just hate a sickening couple?"

JANINE SAT cross legged in the middle of the floor, her eyes closed and her hands in prayer position in front of her heart. She sucked in a long deep breath and then blew it out very slowly.

"Take one more deep breath in, hold it at the top and then blow it out. Try to get your exhalation longer than your inhalation," she said to the class. Today there were nine women sitting in front of her, all in the same position with their eyes closed. The feeling of energy in the room was something she always enjoyed.

"Now, open your eyes. Namaste," she said, bowing her head as she ended the last yoga class of the day. She only had two classes a day right now, simply because she didn't have enough students to warrant any more. Business had been good, but it would have to grow a lot more in order for her to maintain the monthly rent and utilities.

Over the last few days, she had calmed down about her fight with William. What was going on with Meg was much more important, obviously. But she missed William. He had come to the family dinner, but they didn't even get a chance to talk before everything happened.

And now she regretted being so ugly to him. Taking criticism had never been something she was good at. Her mother had always been a critical person, so Janine felt a little bit like a scalded dog whenever someone criticized her.

Then there was the added fact that people tended to think that because she taught yoga and meditation, she was somehow stupid. Uneducated. Head in the clouds all the time. And while that was somewhat true in the sense that she didn't have a whole lot of business acumen, she was no dummy.

"Have a good day, ladies," she said, as the last two women walked out the door. She turned around to check her phone for any text messages. She and Julie had been talking a lot back-and-forth about Meg and what to do. She hadn't admitted that she knew for weeks that Meg was pregnant, and she hoped she never had to. That might just completely destroy her relationship with Julie.

"Hi."

She turned around to see William standing there, his hands in the pockets of his jeans, a slight smile on his face. Dang, he was handsome. Her immediate urge was to run to him, grab his adorable cheeks and plant a kiss on his lips. Instead, she stood still.

"Hey."

He took a few steps toward her. "I miss you."

"Do you?" she said, her lips starting to turn up into a smile that she tried desperately to stop.

He walked closer. "More than I could've imagined."

"Well, then, I guess you shouldn't have acted like a horse's ass."

He chuckled. "Is that the way it went?"

"Okay, so maybe I also acted a little badly…"

He closed the distance between them, his face just inches from hers. "Forgive me?" he asked, softly.

"As long as you forgive me," she said, looking up at him. William leaned down and brushed his lips against hers.

"Forgiven."

"Ditto."

He pulled her into a tight embrace, pressing his lips to hers. When they finally came up for air, she smiled up at him.

"I guess this was our first big fight."

"Let's make it our last fight, okay? I haven't slept in days."

Janine giggled. "Okay, no more fights. We'll just be blissfully happy forever and ever."

"Sounds like a plan," he said, stepping back, his arms around her waist. "Looks like you had a pretty full class."

"I did. But, you're right. I have to make some changes to my class rates. I did the numbers, and I'm just not able to offer all that free stuff until I get on my feet."

He grinned. "Did you just say I was right?"

"Don't get used to it," she said, pinching his arm.

# CHAPTER 7

*J*ulie stood in the bookstore, staring off into space out onto the sidewalk. Why did everybody have to look so happy today? She wondered if they had the same kind of problems she had going on in her life right now.

A daughter who left college and was pregnant at nineteen years old.

A "sort of" boyfriend who seemed to be "sort of" dating his high school crush behind her back.

A wretched ex-husband with an even worse fiancée.

And serious writer's block.

For weeks, she had been trying to get back into writing her novel, a semi autobiographical version of her life. But now she felt like her life was becoming so unbelievable that nobody was going to want to read her book.

More than anything, she wanted her daughter to be okay. She wanted her to open up, talk about what she was going through. But so far, Meg seemed to be isolating herself. Thankfully, one bright spot had appeared. Meg had asked her to go to her next doctor's appointment with her.

As she wiped down the counter for the fifteenth time, she thought about how that appointment might go. Would she get to see the baby on ultrasound? Would she get to hear the heartbeat? And would that make everything even harder if Meg chose to give the baby up for adoption?

She turned her back for a moment to pick up a stack of books that needed to be put back in their proper places. The bell on the door dinged, and she turned around to see Christian standing there.

So far, she had been able to avoid him. There was a part of her that blamed him for everything that was going on with her daughter. He was older than her, more experienced, more mature. How had he allowed this to happen?

"Hello, Madame," he said, his thick French accent seeming less appealing than normal.

"Hello." Julie just stood there, cleaning cloth in her hand, unsure of what to say. "Can I help you with something?"

He smiled slightly and looked at his feet. "I thought maybe we could talk."

She nodded slightly toward one of the bistro chairs in the café. Christian walked over and sat down, and she followed. She found herself suddenly wishing for a rush of customers to come into the store so that she could have a reason to tell him to go. But the other part of her really wanted to hear what he was going to say.

"What would you like to talk about?"

"I know this is highly irregular for me to be here. But your daughter won't speak to me, and I don't know what else to do. I'm not leaving until we work this out one way or the other."

"Well, my daughter is an adult in the eyes of the law. I can't force her to talk to you."

"I understand. And I know you must not like me very much."

"On the surface, no. I definitely don't like you. But I don't know you well enough as a person to make a final determination."

"I don't blame you. If I lived thousands of miles away from my daughter and found out she was seeing a man who was older than her, I might feel the same. But I would like you to know that I truly love your daughter."

"So I've heard."

"It may not matter much, but I've always

respected her. We never... Well, I don't really know how to say this to someone's mother..."

Julie put her hand up. "I get it. But I really don't want to hear any more about that."

"Yes. Totally understandable. You must know also that the baby is half of me too. I am very distraught that Meg would come here and possibly give away our baby without me ever knowing."

Julie sucked in a long breath and blew it out. "We can agree on that. I think that was the wrong thing to do."

"I just want to be involved in whatever way I can. I still love your daughter, and my plan was to be with her for the rest of my life. We have a lot in common, although you may not think that's possible. I feel like Meg is an old soul."

Julie laughed softly. "We've always said that about her, actually. And I think it's why she feels things so deeply."

"Yes, she's a very empathetic person. Anyway, I was just hoping that maybe you could talk to her for me. I'd like to sit down and discuss the situation, maybe even be involved in the doctor's appointments. I just want her to hear me out."

"As I said, I can't force my daughter to do anything, but I will speak with her. Encourage her to talk to you so that she can get some closure."

He nodded slightly, a sad look on his face. "I hope

this isn't the end for us. I've never met a woman like your daughter, and I dare say I will never meet another one like her again."

"I have work to do, so if there's nothing else?"

"Yes, I don't want to interfere with your work day. Thank you for listening to me," he said, standing up.

Julie nodded and walked back up to the front of the store as Christian walked out the door. Before leaving, he turned around and looked at her.

"I don't know if you've ever been in love. I assume you have. Not being with Meg is ripping out my heart, and I'll do anything to stop feeling like this. I hope she'll speak with me soon."

With that, he walked down the sidewalk, and Julie was left feeling conflicted. This man actually seemed to love her daughter, and now she didn't know what to think.

MEG SAT at the large conference table alone. Even though she had support available, she felt like this was something she needed to do by herself. She told no one she was coming here, not wanting to hear everyone else's opinions. It was so hard to keep herself objective about the situation, especially with the baby starting to kick. Feeling all of that made her even more determined to make the right decision, but it also ripped her heart out when she even considered handing her baby over to strangers in a few months.

A woman walked into the room, prim and proper in her business suit. Meg didn't have any maternity clothes yet, mainly because she had been trying to hide her pregnancy for so long. Today, she wore her biggest pair of sweat pants and an oversized pink sweater. She was hot, moody and uncomfortable. Maternity clothes were definitely something on her list that she needed to get.

The woman sat down, a stack of file folders in her hand. "Hello, Meg. It's very nice to meet you. I'm Lucinda Clark. I'm the adoptive parent coordinator."

Meg reached her hand across the table to shake Lucinda's. Everything about this woman looked put together. Not a hair out of place. Expensive designer suit, make up that made every blemish disappear, beautiful and perfect white teeth. Meg felt like a troll that lived under a bridge sitting across from her.

"Nice to meet you."

"So, I understand that you're considering adoption. I just want you to know that it's a very selfless thing to do, to give your child the opportunity for a better home and to give a family the ability to grow. I also understand that you're currently undecided, and that's totally normal. This is a big decision. A lot of our birthmothers go back-and-forth and don't make a final decision even up until the baby is born."

"Oh no. I don't want to do that. I want to make a final decision as soon as possible because this is really tearing me apart. My family wants me to keep the baby, as does the birth father."

Lucinda looked at her carefully. "The birth father? I wasn't aware that he was involved."

"Well, he wasn't until recently. He's a French citizen, and I got pregnant over there while I was at college. He came here to find me a few days ago, so he's here in town."

"That does complicate things, Meg. A birth father has rights, and I'll have to talk to our attorneys to figure out exactly what they are since he is not a US citizen."

"I understand. I just thought since I haven't actually even made the decision yet, maybe I could come and look at some of the adoptive family files. You know, see if anybody feels right to me. Then I can talk to the birth father."

Lucinda nodded her head and slid a few file folders over to Meg. "Alright, that sounds good. If at all possible, we would want his agreement just to make everything legal."

"Of course."

"I've taken the liberty of pulling a few files that I think fit what you're looking for. All are two parent homes, and all of them are open to sending photos and updates throughout the years."

"I'm not sure I even want that, honestly. I think it's going to make everything much harder."

"I understand you have a lot of conflicting feelings right now. We can decide those sorts of things later. Honestly, most adoptive families are open to whatever contact you're comfortable with, even if it's none."

Meg let out a breath she had been holding. "Good."

"Well, I'll leave you to it. When you're finished, you can just give those folders to my assistant on the way out. Take as much time as you need, and call me if you see a family that you would like to meet with."

Lucinda stood up, touched Meg's shoulder and walked out of the room. Meg had never felt so alone. How was she supposed to choose strangers to raise her baby? What if everything they wrote about themselves was a lie?

She carefully opened the first folder. There was a paper on the front that was a letter to the birth mother. Attached were pictures of the couple. There was also home study information inside detailing what kind of house they had, jobs and other pertinent information.

The first couple seemed nice enough. The husband was an architect, the wife was planning to be a homemaker. They lived in Atlanta and had no children. They did have a cat, and Meg didn't like cats. She was allergic. She closed the folder and pushed it away, not wanting to risk that her baby was going to have the same allergies that she did. It was the first motherly decision she had made.

She opened the second folder. It had the same set up, only this time the couple was a little bit younger. They lived in North Carolina and had two kids, three dogs and loved to raise chickens. Meg rolled her eyes, shook her head and pushed the folder away. The last thing she wanted was to put her baby in a household that already had kids. No, she wanted her child to get undivided attention, at least for the first year or so. And she definitely didn't want her baby to have to compete for attention with a bunch of chickens.

She opened the third file folder and saw a very pleasant looking couple. They seemed to probably be in their late twenties, not that much older than her. But they certainly had their lives together a lot more than she did.

They lived in Orlando, and the husband was a marketing executive. The wife was a schoolteacher. They had a basset hound and no kids. Heck, Meg thought she might want to go live with them.

She read their birthmother letter. It was heartfelt, and she got a good feeling about them. They were open to as much contact as she wanted to have. They had been trying to get pregnant for three years but then found out that the wife needed a hysterectomy. Their only option at this point would be adoption.

Meg felt an immediate conflict in her gut. A part of her wanted to keep her child no matter what. Another part of her wanted to give her baby the best possible life, and wouldn't that be with a couple like this? She couldn't provide anything near what this couple could. Well, except for the love she had.

Every day, it was getting harder and harder to feel detached from the life growing inside of her. Now that the baby was moving more, she felt every kick and flutter. And she felt a growing love in her heart that she had never experienced before. A mother's love, she assumed.

If she gave her baby up for adoption, she wouldn't get to make all of those parental decisions as the years went by. The only decision she would get to make was whether or not to give her baby to someone else to raise.

And she wanted to make the best decision. If it was her only decision, she wanted it to be a good one.

She closed the folder and put her head on the table. She had prayed more since being pregnant than she had in her entire life. She just wanted God to send a really obvious sign on what she should do, but so far she hadn't felt pulled one way or the other. Some moments she was adamantly against adoption, and other moments she felt like it was the only good solution.

And then there was Christian. She had to talk to him, she knew that. She had been avoiding it mainly because she loved him so much. She knew that when they met, he would likely try to talk her into keeping the baby, and she just didn't want to feel pressured.

On the other hand, it wasn't fair to him. He had a right to have an opinion.

She stood up and walked over to the window which looked out over the city. Off in the distance, she could see the island. She thought about what it would be like to raise a child in this area, next to the wild marshes and the beautiful ocean. What an idyllic childhood that could be.

Conflicted, she turned, picked up the folders and handed them to the assistant before getting on the elevator. As she stood there, still unsure of what to do, she prayed that God would give her a sign, some way of knowing that if she kept her baby everything would be all right. Or, some way of knowing that her baby was meant to be with another family.

"Wow, you do have a lot going on," Tucker said as they walked down the beach.

Colleen had found him to be a great confidante, after all he didn't know anyone she was talking about anyway.

"Yeah, it's been a whirlwind."

"What do you think your sister will decide?"

Colleen sighed. "I don't know, honestly. But, I hope she keeps the baby. I just can't imagine never knowing my niece or nephew."

"That's hard. You know, I'm adopted."

Colleen stopped walking. "Really?"

"Yeah. I was adopted at three days old. In fact, my birthmother left me at a fire station."

Her heart dropped. What must that be like, to know you were abandoned?

"Wow. I'm so sorry," she said, not really knowing what to say.

Tucker smiled. "I'm over it now."

"Did you ever find out why?"

"Yeah. About a year ago, I hired a private investigator. My mother had been fifteen years old when she got pregnant. She didn't have a good family situation, and she hid her pregnancy. Gave birth to me alone in a vacant house and left me at the fire station. She watched from the woods across the street for hours until she was sure someone found me."

"Oh my gosh, Tucker. She must have been devastated. I cannot imagine."

"Not everyone has a good family situation. It makes me appreciate the great family I have now. Family doesn't have to be blood."

They started walking again. "You're right. But, Meg has our support, one hundred percent."

"True. But, this is her baby. Her flesh and blood. And she has to decide what's best. I know it's hard, but give her space. Let her know you're there, but don't judge whatever she decides. That baby will be loved no matter where it ends up."

In her heart, she knew he was right, but the selfish part of her still wanted Meg to keep the baby. Why were things always so hard?

# CHAPTER 8

*J*anine and Julie walked down the sidewalk, looking in the shop windows. Although they had invited Meg to go with them, she said she was tired and wanted to rest up for her doctor's appointment that afternoon.

But she was running out of clothing quickly. Her sweaters were starting to become tight, and Julie was getting tired of seeing her walk around in sweatpants all the time.

"So, you haven't talked to Dawson this week?"

"He's called and texted a few times, but I told him I was just really busy with all of this going on with Meg."

"Maybe it wasn't what you thought. I mean, maybe he was just having lunch with an old friend."

Julie stopped and looked at her sister. "Really? If

it's no big deal, then why is he hiding it? Why does he keep telling me that he's just got some important job he's working on?"

Janine shrugged her shoulders. "I don't know. Men are impossible."

Julie laughed. "Well, I've been through a lot worse, and I'm not getting hurt like that again. I'd rather be alone."

They continued walking until they came to the maternity shop. They went inside, searched through the racks and found some suitable basic clothes they could get for Meg. After making sure she could return them if they didn't fit, Julie paid for the items and they left the store.

"Want to grab a cup of coffee?" Janine asked.

"I thought you had a class soon?"

"Not for a couple of hours. And I hate sitting at the studio all alone. It's kind of depressing."

"Where is William?"

"He had some business in Charleston today. So, I'd much rather get coffee with my sister if she's agreeable," she said, smiling.

The two women walked a block over to the coffee shop. Julie loved this place. It was very down home and laid back. She hated those big coffee chains with a passion. Although, when she had lived in Atlanta, she'd frequented them often, most of the time with unlikable women from the country club.

They sat down at a table after getting their coffee, and Janine looked at her sister.

"I know you're worried about Meg."

"How could I not be? You haven't told Mom have you?"

"Are you crazy? There's no way I would tell her! I think we should just keep it between us until we know what Meg is going to do. And, if she keeps the baby, I don't think we should tell Mom until the kid is at least ten years old," Janine said, with a laugh.

Julie smiled. "*If she keeps it*. I absolutely hate saying that phrase."

Janine smiled sadly. "I know. It's just hard to fathom that she might choose adoption. I mean, I believe in adoption whole heartedly. But I can't even imagine the thought that she would give her baby away."

"I just don't think she's thinking clearly. And the very fact that someone else knew that she was pregnant and didn't tell me…"

Janine froze in her seat, her hands gripping her cup of coffee for dear life. Her eyes were wide, and her face seemed to lose its color quickly.

"Wait. You know about that?"

"Yes, I know," Julie said. "And, at first I was very angry about it. But the more I thought about it, the more I understood."

Janine blew out a relieved breath. "Wow. I wasn't

expecting that kind of reaction. I really thought you would be angry, and maybe it might even ruin our relationship."

"Our relationship? Why would..." Julie started to say. Then her brain cells all started connecting together. "Are you telling me that you knew?"

Janine swallowed hard, her mouth hanging open for a moment. "I thought that's what you were saying..."

"I found out that Dixie knew a few days before I found out. But you knew also?"

Janine buried her head in her hands. "Oh no..."

"Answer me, Janine," Julie said, her voice shaking with anger.

"Julie, you have to know that I didn't intend for this to happen."

She couldn't believe it. All those years that they didn't speak happened because Janine had butted into her relationship with her daughters, and now she had gone and done it all over again.

"How long have you known?" Julie asked, her voice monotone and restrained. They were in a public place, and she really didn't feel like getting arrested for disorderly conduct today.

"I've known since shortly after she got here. I overheard her talking on the phone, making a doctor's appointment. I confronted her about it that morning and ended up going to the appointment with her."

Julie started to cry, something she did when she got angry enough. It was an irritating personality trait. The very moment she wanted to be strong, but she couldn't stop bawling.

"You went to her appointment?"

"I thought someone should…"

"Yes! Her *mother*! You're not her mother, Janine!"

"Julie, please, try to understand…"

"I trusted you. I thought we had a new relation-ship, and you do this to me?"

"I didn't mean to do anything. I told her to tell you. I begged her."

"Why didn't you tell me?"

"Because it wasn't my secret to tell."

"Gosh, I'm getting tired of people saying that to me. I'm the mother! This is my child! How could you go for weeks and not tell me? How could you sit and have dinner and coffee and go shopping and never tell me?"

"I was so worried about Meg, and she swore me to secrecy. She just wanted time to think through her options, and I thought I should give her that."

Julie stood up, picked up the shopping bag and stepped away from the table. "Keep your nose out of my daughter's business. And maybe you should start looking for another place to live."

With that, she walked down the sidewalk without looking back.

DAWSON STOOD in the middle of the room and took a long sip of his water. It had been a hotter than normal day, and he wasn't feeling himself anyway. Contracting work was tough, and the older he got, the more he wondered how long he could do it. Tarps were strewn around the old house, and new appliances were still covered sitting in the kitchen.

His relationship with Julie was up in the air right now, and he was trying hard to give her the space she needed. Her daughter's pregnancy seemed to have brought the family to a halt, and every time he tried to talk to her, she brushed him off. She was in a rush or too busy to see him. And his work schedule seemed to be a sore subject with her too. The last thing he needed was for her to find out his client was Tiffany.

The more time he spent with Tiffany, the more thankful he was that things had never worked out between them. A high school crush was one thing, but the woman was nauseating to be around. He'd thought long and hard about telling Julie who his new client was, but decided she didn't need the extra stress. In his eyes, it was better to just get the job done and move on with his new life with Julie.

But now he wondered if she even wanted that. She had pulled back so much that he feared she wasn't interested in him anymore. He decided to let her come to him since she obviously needed her space.

"It's shaping up nicely, don't you think?" Tiffany said as she breezed through her shambles of a living room for the twentieth time that day. She was a control freak, and it was grating on his last nerve.

"Yep," Dawson said, under his breath as he went back to painting the wall for the third time. She'd changed her mind about the paint color so many times that he was getting embarrassed to go to the paint store.

"Blaine's money spends much better than mine," she said, giggling like a crazy person. After running into Tiffany at the reunion and exchanging contact info for her renovation project, Dawson had learned that she and Blaine divorced a year ago, and she took him to the cleaners, as they say. She got most of his money and one of their houses. Of course, after seeing a late night infomercial, she decided to become a real estate investor. And she was a terrible one.

Bossy. Uninformed. Uneducated. Mouthy. Argumentative. There just weren't enough adjectives to describe how much he wished he hadn't taken the job.

"My guy will get those appliances installed tomorrow. Once I finish up the painting in here, we'll move to the master bedroom."

She smiled and made a purring noise. "Wow, I never thought I'd hear Dawson Lancaster say we could move to the master bedroom." Tiffany walked by and rubbed his upper arm as she moved to the other side of him.

"Tiffany, I told you to stop saying stuff like that. I have a girlfriend." He didn't know if he really did, but he sure wasn't interested in her no matter what.

"Really? That mousy little thing from the reunion? She can't hold the attention of a man like you."

Now, he was mad. "Okay, you listen up, Tiffany. I'm doing this renovation job because it's my business. I won't be discussing my personal life with you, and I don't want to hear your opinions about anything. Got it?"

She poked her bottom lip out, which looked incredibly ridiculous for a forty year old woman, but then again so did those knee high fringe boots she was wearing. "Don't be rude, Dawson. It's unbecoming."

He rolled his eyes and went back to painting. For the life of him, he couldn't understand why any sane teenage boy had a crush on her back in the day. Hormones were a funny thing.

"I think I'm about finished here for today," he said, putting the roller down and turning toward the door.

"Wait, Dawson. I'm sorry I offended you. Why don't we go into Charleston and get some lunch?"

"No, thanks. I'm going to go fishing and then see Julie, if she'll see me."

"If she'll see you? Is she crazy?"

"Tiffany, enough. I'll be back tomorrow morning, bright and early." Without another word, he gathered his things and walked out the door.

JULIE TAPPED her foot as they waited for the doctor to come into the room. Meg looked so tiny sitting on the table wearing the paper gown. How, in all the decades of medical technology, had they not developed something better than a tiny, ill-fitting paper gown to cover women? These were the beings that brought life into the world; didn't they deserve fabric or something more comfortable?

As she watched her daughter, who was checking social media on her phone, she remembered when she was young, having to take her to pediatrician appointments. Meg had childhood asthma, so they spent a lot of time together sitting in examining rooms, and Meg didn't look much bigger now than she did then. Well, except for the growing belly that protruded from her midsection.

"Why are doctors always running late?" Meg said, groaning. The age old question.

"Because they know we'll wait no matter what," Julie said, honestly.

"I'm nervous."

"Why? Things have been going well so far. No reason to think this appointment will be any different, honey," Julie said as she mindlessly flipped through a magazine, not really reading any of the words.

"No, I mean about the delivery. It's getting closer, and it's starting to freak me out. I watched some videos online…"

"Oh, sweetie," Julie said, standing up and rubbing her leg. "Don't watch videos. That will terrify you. Childbirth isn't pretty."

"It was like a horror movie, Mom. I never saw it from that… angle… before."

Julie smiled. "Listen, they have wonderful drugs for that."

"Have you seen an epidural needle? It's twenty feet long!"

Julie tried not to laugh at that description.

"You're going to do just fine, Meg. You're strong, and we'll take this one step at a time."

"Sorry to keep you waiting, folks," the doctor said as she breezed into the room. "Doctor Hodges is on vacation. I'm Doctor Wells."

"Hi. I'm Meg and this is my mother, Julie."

"Nice to meet you," Julie said, reaching out her hand. The doctor smiled and nodded.

"Sorry, I can't shake your hand. Already put my gloves on," she said, smiling.

"Of course."

"So, how are you feeling, Meg?"

"Fat."

The doctor laughed. "I hear that a lot. Any issues?"

"Gas, belching and mood swings."

"I hear that a lot too. I can give you some literature on how to help with the gas and belching, but I'm afraid the mood swings are going to remain. It gets a lot better in the third trimester for most women. You're almost there."

"Thank goodness."

"Any pain or bleeding?"

"No."

"Excellent. Have you been taking your pre-natal vitamins regularly?"

"Yes. And avoiding caffeine."

"Great. Let's go ahead and take some measurements, and then we'll listen to your sweet baby's heartbeat."

As the doctor moved around Meg's belly, Julie thought about her words. "Sweet baby". There was a tiny little human growing inside of her daughter, completely dependent on her to make decisions. Julie prayed that whatever decision was made would be the right one for the baby.

"You're measuring right on target," the doctor said. "Let's take a listen to the baby's heartbeat." She pulled out a portable device and moved it around Meg's stomach until she found the heartbeat. It was fast, as baby's heartbeats normally were. Meg smiled when she heard it. "Have you been feeling the baby move?"

"Yes. A lot more in the last couple of weeks."

"Well, that will increase even more when you pass twenty-five weeks. Get ready to be elbowed and kicked from the inside," she said, laughing.

"I remember when I was pregnant with you," Julie said. "You were my most active baby. Constantly kicking and twirling around."

"Really?" Meg said as she sat up.

"Oh yes. Of course, you were the same way after you were born, so I wasn't surprised."

Meg laughed, and Julie was so excited to see that. It was the first time in a long time she'd seen her daughter happy, even if it was just for a fleeting moment.

"Well, that's all for today. We'll schedule your glucose screening test for two weeks from now."

"What's that?"

"We just want to make sure you're at low risk for gestational diabetes."

"Pregnancy is way more complicated than I realized," Meg said as she stepped off the table.

"Wait until you get to parenting," the doctor said, laughing, as she looked at Julie for agreement. Julie froze in place. "Oh. Jeez. I'm so sorry, Meg. I totally forgot you were considering…"

"It's okay."

"I'd better get to my next patient. Call me if you need anything, and you can check out up front. Nice to meet you, Julie."

The doctor left the room, and Julie turned around to give Meg privacy while she changed back into her clothes. "So, when can you find out the sex of the baby?"

"I already have it in a sealed envelope."

Julie was surprised. "Really?"

"Yeah, but I'm not sure I want to know," she said. "You can turn around now."

She stood there in her new maternity jeans and flowy top that Julie had bought for her earlier in the day, and she looked so mature, so grown up. It made Julie's eyes water a bit.

"It's your decision, honey. No pressure."

They checked out and walked through the parking lot of the large medical building toward Julie's car. Meg was quiet, but finally spoke.

"Listen, Aunt Janine told me what happened today."

Julie's jaw tightened. "She shouldn't have said anything to you. This is between me and my sister."

Meg stopped. "Mom, look, this is all my fault. I should've told you first. I get that. But when she guessed, I was relieved that someone knew. I needed someone who loved me to be there."

"That should've been me, Meg. I'm your mother. No one loves you more than I do." She struggled to hold back her tears.

Meg put her hand on Julie's arm. "This isn't Janine's fault. I put her in an impossible situation, Mom. I begged her not to tell, and she begged me to tell you several times. She risked her relationship with you to give me the peace I needed for a few weeks. She took care of me in your place, even though she was against it the whole time."

"It hurt, honey. To know I was the last person you trusted…"

"No. That wasn't it. You were the last person I wanted to disappoint."

Julie hugged her. "You could never disappoint me, Meg. I love you, and I love that baby."

Meg pulled back. "Are you still going to love me if I decide not to keep this baby?"

Julie nodded, a few tears escaping her eyes. "Of course, I will. No matter what. That's what mothers do."

And with that, Julie put her arm around her daughter and walked to her car, praying that she said the right words and that her daughter would come through this whole ordeal a better, stronger woman.

MEG STARED off into space as she waited for Christian to arrive at the restaurant. She'd chosen a place on the water, mainly to give herself the serenity of the ocean view. She was more stressed out than she'd ever been in her life, and working up the courage to face Christian again was one of the hardest things she'd ever done.

"Hello," he said, softly, as he sat down across from her.

"Hey."

"I was happy that you texted me. Honestly, I was starting to worry that you never would."

"I just didn't know what to say."

"And now?"

"I still don't. Look, I never meant to hurt you. You know I adore you."

He reached across and took her hand. "And I adore you. Which is why you broke my heart so easily, Meg. I've never felt about anyone the way I feel about you."

"I didn't want to risk your job, and I didn't want you to feel obligated," she said, finally looking him in the eyes.

"How could you think I would feel that way? Obligation is not something I feel about this situation at all. If that were the case, I wouldn't have traveled all the way here to ask you if you were carrying my child."

"You're a good man, Christian. I knew you'd do the right thing even if it threw your whole life off track. Do you know what a great career you have in front of you? If the administration found out a student was pregnant by a professor, even though you weren't my professor... well, it'd be on the local news! You'd lose everything you worked for. And for what? Me?"

Christian's eyes widened. "You act as if you're not worth valuing, my darling. But you're everything to me, and that baby you're carrying was conceived in love. You know this."

"I do know, but you have a chance to have your dream life. I'm staying here, no matter what. My family is here. And even if I give up the baby, my life will never be the same."

Christian hung his head. "How can you even think of giving our child to strangers? Please understand that I can't accept that, Meg. I love you and this baby. We can be a family."

Tears fell down her cheeks. "I want that more than anything," she said. "But you live in France, Christian. Your whole life and career are there. It isn't fair to ask you to uproot everything just because I forgot to take my pills."

"This baby was meant to be here, Meg. I believe this with my whole heart. Please don't make any rash decisions yet, okay? Let me be a part of this. Let me feel my baby kick and hear the heartbeat and see the ultrasounds. Give me that much."

"It will only make it worse if I decide to pursue the adoption."

"Let's not talk about that just now, okay? For this moment, let's see what it would be like to be a family. Will you do this for me?"

She never could say no to his beautiful French accent.

"Fine. We'll play family. I'll take you to my next appointment. You can feel my belly all you want. But, I'm not making any promises."

# CHAPTER 9

*J*anine sat in her room, looking around at the very few belongings that she actually owned. It wouldn't take her long to pack up and leave, just like Julie told her to. She could have pretty much everything in one suitcase and be out within the hour.

But she didn't have anywhere to go. And she didn't want to leave like this.

She sat on her bed, thumbing through the only photo album she had. Pictures from her childhood, from all of her travels and pictures of her and Julie as kids brought back tons of memories. She looked at one photo, from her tenth birthday party, where she and Julie were running through a sprinkler in their backyard. As she closed her eyes, she could smell the freshly cut grass and hear the laughter of all of her friends. Those were such simple times. She hated for their relationship to break apart all over again like this.

But it was her own fault. She knew in her heart that she shouldn't have kept the secret, but she felt like she had been put in an impossible situation. At least now everything was out in the open.

She stood up and pulled her only suitcase out of the closet. As she started packing everything, she thought about where she would go. She didn't have much money yet from her business, so she would have to stay in a room or maybe a cheap hotel until she could figure out her next move. She'd have to stay local, which would mean she and Julie would run into each other all the time. But there was no way she was giving up her brand new business and relationship with William.

Of course, William had offered to let her come stay with him, but she didn't feel right doing that. Their relationship was new, and she didn't want to take things to that level just yet.

She folded her clothes neatly, placing them in the suitcase. She walked over to the bathroom to get some of her toiletries and found Julie standing in the hallway outside of her door.

"Oh. I didn't know you were home. I'm just finishing my packing." Without saying another word, she turned around and walked back into her bedroom. Julie followed her and shut the door. She just stood there, without any words.

"You don't have to leave."

"Apparently, I do," Janine said, sitting down on the edge of her bed. Julie crossed her arms.

"It turns out that maybe I overreacted."

"Really? That almost never happens."

"Look, Janine, I don't want to lose our relationship over this. We know how this happened before, and we almost lost each other forever. You're my sister. And I love you."

"I love you too," Janine said, a tear falling from her eye. "And I'm so sorry that I kept a secret from you."

Julie walked closer as Janine stood. They hugged each other for a long moment.

"I just got upset, and I said some things I shouldn't have."

"No, I deserved it."

Julie smiled. "Where did you think you were going, anyway?"

"Well, I'm not sure. I thought about a hotel, but there was a good chance I was gonna sleep in the treehouse Dawson has on his uncle's property."

The two women laughed. Janine was so happy that she didn't have to leave, and that Julie had forgiven her. That showed real growth in their relationship.

"So, how did the doctor appointment go?"

They both sat down on the end of the bed. "It went well. It's just so hard imagining that my daughter may give her baby away. It literally makes me sick to my stomach to think of some other woman getting to be the grandmother."

"Don't lose hope. I think she's just going through a swirl of emotions, and she might surprise you in the end."

"I hope so. She had dinner with Christian tonight, but I don't know how that went. I think she's already asleep in her room."

"We have a lot more time before this baby is going to be born. We just have to show her what a wonderful, supportive family she has. She's not some teenage girl alone. She needs to know we have her back," Janine said.

"You're right. We just have to make her see that she can do this and that we will help her because we're family."

"ENJOY YOUR BOOK," Julie said as she rang up a customer. The woman had purchased an organic gardening book, saying she was going to plant her own garden and learn how to compost. Julie thought about how it must be nice to have such simple things to think about because these days every one of her thoughts seemed way too complicated.

As the woman walked out of the store, Dawson walked in. No one else was there, Dixie having gone to one of her Parkinson's therapy sessions. Feeling a bit like a cornered rat, Julie tried to act normal.

"Hello, stranger," he said with a smile.

"Hey. How's everything going?" She really didn't know what to say, and for some reason the whole thing felt very uncomfortable.

Julie had spent a lot of time thinking over the last couple of days about whether they were even dating or not. To be grownups, neither of them were very good at this whole relationship thing.

"I figured if I wanted to see you, I'd better just show up at your work. You seem to be really hard to get on text or phone lately," he said.

"Yeah, sorry about that. I've just been really wrapped up in this whole thing with Meg. Did you need something?"

He furrowed his eyebrows and cocked his head. "Yeah, I need *you*."

She wasn't getting reeled in. No way, no how. He had no idea she had seen him with Tiffany, and she preferred to keep it that way. She wasn't about to make herself look like some sort of desperate, jealous woman – even if that's what she was right now.

Every time she thought about the moment she saw him with Tiffany, it made her think of Michael. She knew it wasn't fair to compare Dawson to her ex-husband, but it was hard not to do that. After all, it'd been less than a year since Michael had ripped her heart to shreds, and now she was faced with going through the same thing again? No, thank you.

"That's a sweet thing to say," she said, smiling slightly.

"Is something wrong?"

"No. I've been meaning to talk to you, though." Julie pointed at the chair at the bistro table as she took a seat across from him. She was going to have to just rip off the bandage.

"This sounds ominous."

"I just wanted to let you know that I think we might need to take a break. " She cleared her throat and tried to avoid eye contact. She was afraid if she looked at his dimples, she might just lose all of her strength.

"A break? What do you mean?"

"Well, there's just a lot going on in my family right now, and I don't think I have time to devote to a relationship. I mean... if that's what this is," she said pointing back-and-forth between the two of them.

Dawson looked at her quizzically. "Did I do something wrong?"

She laughed it off. "No, of course not. It's just that I'm exhausted between work and dealing with this whole thing with Meg.

"I guess I just thought I could be helpful to you going through all of this. I didn't expect that you would want to take time apart." He looked truly upset, which made Julie feel bad except that she knew that he had been spending time with Tiffany. He had obviously been keeping it from her, and even though she wanted to keep seeing him, she didn't want to go through that kind of hurt all over again. She didn't want to be anyone's second choice, back up girlfriend.

With Michael, it had been devastating because it came out of left field. They had spent over two decades together. She figured, even though she had strong feelings for Dawson, it couldn't possibly hurt as much if she broke things off early in the relationship.

"We're still friends, Dawson. I just don't have the mental space right now to be committing to much more than that. My daughter needs me."

"Why do I get the feeling something else is going on?"

"I don't know. I'm being perfectly honest with you."

"It doesn't seem like you are. I just don't get it.

We were enjoying our time together, and I thought things were heading in a certain direction…"

"Things have changed, Dawson. My whole life is in flux right now. I don't even know if Meg is keeping my grandchild, for goodness sakes. It's a lot to deal with."

"I want to be there for you," he said, softly. Her heart was breaking.

"Then be there as my friend." She wanted to throw up. That wasn't what she wanted at all, but pride is a strong thing.

He sucked in a sharp breath and blew it out. "Got it," he said, standing up. "If you need me, you know where to find me."

She almost wanted to run after him for some inexplicable reason. But at the same time, she knew she was right. He was hiding his secret relationship with Tiffany from her. He was obviously sneaking around behind her back, so why should she be the one feeling bad?

Maybe she should've confronted him, made him feel horrible for stringing her along while chasing after Tiffany. But she didn't want to give him the satisfaction of thinking he had upset her. Never again was she going to allow a man to have that kind of power over her.

She walked to the window and watched him as he disappeared around the corner and out of sight.

Although it hurt, it couldn't possibly hurt as much as waiting even another day to break things off. So why did she feel so incredibly bad?

MEG STOOD outside of the ice cream shop, a cone with two scoops of chocolate teetering in her hand. She just couldn't help herself lately. The cravings had become too much.

Over the last week, she'd found herself craving pickles with peanut butter, chicken noodle soup, crackers with spray cheese and a whole host of other non-delectable items she wasn't expecting. This was a far cry from the beautiful, rich foods she'd enjoyed in France. What she wouldn't give for a big baguette and a hunk of cheese right now.

She'd agreed to meet Christian and spend some time together. If she was being honest with herself, she was looking forward to it. She missed him and all of the time they had spent together back in Europe.

But now she had to be practical. She knew his main focus would be to get her to keep the baby, and she still hadn't made up her mind. Of course, she knew he had the right to an opinion about the baby's future also. They would have to agree, and she wasn't sure that was even possible.

There were times that she laid in bed at night and tried to imagine being a mother. Taking her child to the playground. Rocking her baby to sleep. Doing all of those fun things that new moms get to do like making bottles and changing diapers and cleaning spit up off of their shoulders. Well, maybe not fun but certainly memorable.

She hadn't even really done a lot of babysitting as a teenager. Her experience with a child was pretty much next to zero, yet she felt an attachment that grew every single day. Every little flutter and kick, and probably even gas bubbles, meant the world to her.

When she found herself thinking about handing her baby over, it made her heart hurt. She couldn't imagine doing it, yet she knew she had to consider it. It felt like the mature thing to do.

Never could she have imagined that she would be in this predicament. She had always been so safety conscious about everything in her life, and yet she had been so careless about her birth control pills.

Still, it didn't feel like a mistake. This was a human being, a gift from God, a sweet little life that was depending on her. And right now, it desperately wanted chocolate ice cream.

"Sorry I'm late," Christian said as he walked around the corner. He looked flustered but excited about something. Probably because he was getting a chance to see her and the baby.

"No problem. This ice cream cone has been keeping me busy," Meg said, smiling. It was nice to feel normal for a change. Now that her secret was out in the open, it made it a lot more comfortable to walk around in the world. That and the fact that her mother had bought her some maternity clothes, so now she was starting to get looks and comments from strangers on the street. Any day now, she knew she would have people asking when she was due.

"I had a meeting that ran long."

They started to walk down the sidewalk toward the bistro where they were going to have an early dinner together.

"A meeting? You don't even know anyone in town."

Christian smiled broadly. "I do now."

"What's going on? You're acting awfully strange."

"Well, I have some big news. I've spent the last week talking to some colleagues over at the local university. And they have offered me a position teaching French history. I can start next semester!"

Meg stopped and looked at him, her eyes wide. "What? Why on earth would you do something like that?"

"Because I want to be here. Surely, that doesn't surprise you."

"But you could've talked to me about it! Christian, I haven't made any decisions yet. And I know you're telling me that you're moving here for me and the baby, but…"

"No. I'm moving here for *you*, and you only. While I hope that we get to keep the baby, I will be here for you no matter what."

Her heart, which lately had felt like a big block of ice, started to melt a bit. Maybe he was telling the truth. Maybe he really would've followed her no matter what.

"And what happens if I decide to go through with the adoption?"

"I'll be heartbroken. I can guarantee you that I'll cry for a long time. But I will love you through it, and I will stand by you. No matter what."

Yep, now her heart really was melting. Was this guy for real? She knew how wonderful he was back in Europe, but this just took it to a whole new level. And now she had more questions swirling around in her brain than ever.

COLLEEN WALKED down the path to the beach, her heart fluttering a bit. When Tucker had asked her out for an official date, she had assumed they would go to a restaurant. Instead, he had asked her to meet him on the beach, in the same place where he had nearly scared her half to death that night.

The sun was just going down, leaving streaks of orange and pink across the sky. She loved the smell of the ocean, the salty sea air blowing on her face as she made her way down onto the beach.

When she came over the crest of one of the dunes, she saw a huge blanket spread out on the sand, an ice bucket with a bottle of wine, candles lit all around and a smiling Tucker standing there.

No one had ever done anything like that for her before. The most Peter had done was make reservations at the fanciest Italian restaurant in town. But Peter mostly did things for show, including having her on his arm.

"Wow. This is amazing!" A part of her was hesitant to get back into a relationship with someone so soon, but her grandmother had always said to strike while the iron was hot, and that was exactly what she was doing. Men like Tucker didn't come along every day. She had to at least try, didn't she? After all, she was young and had her whole life in front of her.

"So you like it?" he asked, a smile on his face.

"Like it? I love it. This is amazing! How did you ever put this together so quickly?"

"Well, I had a good education from my mother. She taught me well when I was a kid how to treat a woman once I started dating. It also helped that my dad was always planning these super romantic dates for my mom. They have always been like two teenagers in love."

Colleen smiled. "We should all be so lucky."

"Truer words were never spoken. Please, have a seat."

Colleen sat down on the blanket as Tucker joined her. There was a large picnic basket in the middle, complete with a blue and red plaid interior. She felt like she had landed right in the middle of a magazine shoot.

"I hope you like the food I picked. I got it catered by the bistro because I know you love it there."

He pulled out several containers. One was her favorite apple walnut chicken salad, and then there was fresh bread. He also had potato salad and baked beans, a Southern staple. For dessert, he had peach cobbler, which was one of Colleen's favorite things on earth.

"You've really outdone yourself," she said, smiling. She felt like a giddy schoolgirl on her first date. Although her first date had not been nearly as romantic. Leo Holmstead had taken her to the local burger joint and then to a dollar movie. Not exactly the kind of date that sweeps a girl off her feet.

"You deserve it. I know you've been really stressed out about work and this situation with your sister. It was the least I could do."

"Well, it's much appreciated. I have to admit, I have felt a little left behind in my family lately. Aunt Janine is busy with her new business, my Mom is focused on my sister and my sister is growing a human being, so I don't really have a lot of interesting things to say at the dinner table."

He looked at her, a quirk of a smile on his face. "I'm always interested in you."

Colleen's stomach did a flip flop. She couldn't remember a man ever saying something like that to her, and she felt like she wanted to giggle. Probably not the best thing for a woman in her twenties to do on a date, so she refrained.

"So, how's everything going at work in the toy zone?"she said with a laugh.

"Oh, that reminds me. I have something for you." He turned to his side and reached down into a dark colored tote bag. He pulled out a stuffed bear, probably more plush than any stuffed animal she'd ever seen. It had a big pink bow and huge, adorable eyes.

"For me?"

"Of course. It's a new design we've been working on, so this is the only prototype. One of a kind."

"But it's just a stuffed animal? I thought you made toys?"

He smiled. "Press its stomach."

When she pressed it, the bear started wiggling and stretching in her hands, laughing hysterically.

Colleen was startled and dropped it. "Oh my gosh, that scared me to death!" she said, laughing.

"Yeah, I thought it might startle you," he said, grinning. "I just figured since you've been going through so much lately with your family, maybe this little bear could remind you to laugh through the tough times."

She looked at him, her head cocked to the side. "I don't understand."

"You don't understand what?"

"They just don't make guys like you."

"Guys like me? What does that mean?"

"You're too good to be true. And that's a little terrifying for me."

"Well, I think the same thing about you. So why don't we just decide to be terrified together?"

# CHAPTER 10

*A*s the weeks passed by, Janine was enjoying seeing Meg get bigger and bigger. She still hadn't told anyone what her plans were as far as the adoption, but Julie and Janine were both encouraged that she was spending so much more time with Christian.

He actually seemed to be a really nice guy. The more time they spent around him, the less they noticed any kind of age difference. He was kind, caring and watched over Meg in a way that warmed Janine's heart.

She remembered her first boyfriend, at least her first serious one, back when she was in high school. What she had mistaken for caring turned out to be controlling, and she counted herself lucky having gotten away from him. Last she heard, he'd been arrested a couple of times for domestic violence. Dodged that bullet.

But, when she watched the interactions between Christian and Meg, and knowing that he had come across the ocean and uprooted his entire life for her, it warmed her heart. Maybe there was true love after all.

Tonight, she was thinking even more about true love as William said he had a big surprise for her. He had picked her up at Julie's house and was driving her over the bridge, forcing her to wear a blindfold.

"You know, if we're just going to dinner, this is going to be a really big let down," Janine said with a laugh.

"Don't worry. We're not just going to dinner."

As they drove over the bridge, he started making turns. Janine was totally confused. He seemed to be going in circles, and she tried to pay attention to figure out where they were going.

"Are we lost?"

William chuckled. "No, but I know what kind of brain you have, and I'm pretty sure you're trying to figure out where we're going. So I'm purposely driving in circles to confuse you. You might as well give up."

They continued driving for another few minutes before he finally parked the car.

"Don't take off the blindfold," he said. "And don't even try to peek."

She had to laugh inside thinking about all of the trouble he had gone to for whatever the surprise was.

In reality, she had wanted to just go home and melt into her bed. Teaching three yoga classes a day, six days a week was starting to wear on her a bit. Before long, because of the popularity of her classes, she might even have to hire another yoga teacher to help her. Once she did her accounting at the end of the month, she would know where she was and whether she had the funds to do that.

But she loved it. She was so happy that she had opened the studio. It had done things beyond her wildest dreams. Every day, she looked out at the faces of her students and saw the changes that they were making. She felt like she was really helping their lives. Her new grief yoga classes had been a godsend for so many people, and she was able to offer a discount package for those students, which made her heart smile.

Still, she was tired tonight. And she really wanted to go take a nice long nap, but there was no way she was going to tell William he couldn't take her out for a surprise. Maybe she could get a strong cup of coffee wherever they were going.

He came around to the other side of the car,

opened the door and took her hand. He had told her to dress up a bit, so she had on a long, flowy black sundress. It was now spring time, and the weather was starting to warm. She was so glad to get out of the cooler temperatures. Being a petite, thin person, she didn't have a whole lot of body heat to spare.

He walked her from the car up onto a sidewalk. She had absolutely no idea where she was at this point.

"Don't let me fall,. These sandals are slick," she said, struggling to keep her balance. She had a new appreciation for people who were blind. How in the world did they manage to get around without being terrified all the time?

"Don't worry. I've got you." The more time they spent together, the more serious their relationship became. And she knew he really did have her. He had her back. And that was more than she could say for any other guy she'd dated.

She heard him open the door and they walked inside. Something about this place felt familiar, but she couldn't put her finger on it. Maybe it was the smell? Or just the feeling?

"Okay, here we go," he said. She felt him reach behind her head and untie the blindfold. As it fell from her eyes, she looked around to see all of her friends and family standing in the middle of her studio.

Decorations were everywhere, music was playing and everybody yelled surprise.

"What is this? It's not my birthday," she said under her breath to William.

"Well, this is your grand opening party. We never got to do anything special when you opened this place, and now that you're so successful, I thought we should celebrate that."

She grinned from ear to ear, amazed that anyone had done something so nice like this for her. She hugged him and planted a kiss on his lips. Then she looked around at the faces of all of her friends and family. Julie, Colleen, Meg, Dixie and even Dawson was standing in the corner. He smiled and waved.

"I can't believe you guys did this!" Janine said, smiling as big as she had ever smiled.

There was catered food on tables, a DJ and a makeshift dance floor in the middle of her studio. Other vendors and business owners from town were there, and she had a chance to mingle with each of them.

Every time she looked around, she was so thankful for the people in her life. The relationship with her sister, her nieces and the new man in her life were all such big blessings that she had never anticipated.

As she mingled and chatted with everyone

throughout the night, Janine felt like the most blessed person on the planet.

JULIE WAS SO happy for her sister, but she also felt incredibly uncomfortable that Dawson was there. It had only been a couple of weeks since their conversation at the bookstore, and she missed him more than she could have imagined.

Thoughts of him spending his time with Tiffany were stuck in her head, playing on repeat like some sort of scratched record.

She hadn't seen them around town, and honestly she hadn't seen Tiffany either. Maybe they had gone on a romantic getaway. Why was she doing this to herself? Why was she allowing these upsetting thoughts to overwhelm her brain when she needed to be strong for her daughter?

Her only focus had been on Meg over the last couple of weeks. Their bond had grown stronger, and she had attended another doctor's appointment with her daughter. This time, Christian also came, and he got to listen to the baby's heartbeat. Julie saw tears in his eyes, which he quickly wiped away before Meg could see them.

Life was starting to get into some kind of routine, although it was still different. Meg being up in the air about what to do about the adoption was something that seemed to always be hanging over her head. Nobody could get really excited about the baby or have a baby shower because the decision just hadn't been made.

It was encouraging that Meg hadn't mentioned it lately, though. Julie hoped that meant that she was thinking about keeping the baby, although she wasn't going to press her daughter. The decision was hard enough without pressure from the family.

Christian had taken a job at the local university, and he would be starting during the summer semester. Thankfully, the university in France had let him out of his contract so that he could pursue the opportunity in the United States.

She watched Meg and Christian interact all the time, and she really felt like they were a good match. Instead of worrying that her daughter had made some terrible decision picking an older man, she saw what Meg saw in him. He was kind hearted, laid-back, super intelligent. And best of all, he seemed to really adore her daughter.

That was really all any mother could ask for. She turned her head and looked at Colleen and Tucker in the other corner. They were standing by the table, plates full of food, laughing. Colleen had been happier than she'd ever seen her since meeting Tucker.

He had come to their last Sunday dinner, where Dawson's presence was definitely missed, and had kept the table entertained with stories of all of the different toys he had created and tested over the years. Julie didn't even know his job existed, but she found it highly interesting when he talked about it.

Colleen was starting to look around for another job. Although she liked working at the law firm, the constant domestic violence cases were wearing on her emotionally. She wasn't sure exactly what she wanted to do, but she knew it wasn't that. She didn't want to be what she called a "paper pusher" for the rest of her life, either.

Julie remembered what it was like to be young and have so many opportunities that it caused analysis paralysis. And then, she ended up raising kids and not having much of a career until they were older.

She had enjoyed having her online boutique, which she had closed a few months back, and she was really enjoying writing her first novel. But the bookstore was something that was in her heart. She loved working with Dixie, but mostly she just loved being surrounded by books. She had always loved to read, and the place just felt like her home away from home.

She risked looking across the room at Dawson, who was standing against the wall chatting with the guy who owned the dry cleaning store down the street. Every so often, he would cut his eyes at her, both of them looking away as soon as they made eye contact.

She wished that it had worked out, that they could have been a couple. He was everything she had ever dreamed of in a man, yet she knew that he had feelings for this woman from his past. She wasn't going to get in the middle of that and risk her heart getting broken all over again, although it felt like it was pretty broken right now.

She walked over to the table and poured herself some punch. The party was starting to wind down, and she would be glad to get home, put on her yoga pants and veg out in front of the TV.

"Mind pouring me a cup?" Dawson said from behind her. She would know his voice anywhere, and it made shivers run across her skin.

"Sure," she said. She poured him a cup and handed it to him, trying not to make too much eye contact.

"Meg looks like she's doing well."

"She's doing better. I suppose you met her boyfriend?"

"I did. Seems like a nice guy."

"He is. I think he's good for her."

There was a long pause, both of them unsure of what to say next.

"I miss you," Dawson finally said.

Julie didn't know what to say. "I miss you too."

"I don't know what happened exactly, but I wish you would talk to me."

She smiled sadly. "I told you that I just need to take a break and focus on my daughter, Dawson. I don't know why you can't understand that."

"Because I don't believe it. She seems to be doing fine, and couples don't break up just because there's a problem. That's when you're supposed to come together. "

"Were we really a couple, though?"

He looked surprised. "I thought we were."

"Look, it just didn't work out. I wish it did, trust me. But I can't keep rehashing this with you. It hurts too much." She turned and started to walk away. Dawson touched her arm. She turned around and looked up at him.

"It hurts because we're supposed to be together, Julie. I can't believe you're just throwing all of this away."

She turned and looked back at him. "I can't believe I had to."

As they cleaned up from the party, Julie found herself going over and over her conversation with

Dawson. On one hand, she wanted him to get the message – that things were over. On the other hand, she wanted him to show up outside of her window, holding a boom box over his head and professing his undying love for her. Life is about balance.

Janine continued mingling with the last few people who were there, one from the town council and another woman who was interested in yoga classes. William, who had planned the whole thing, was busy cleaning up, putting folding tables away in the back storage area. Julie felt like the least she could do was help him.

She had sent Meg home to get some rest, with Christian driving her back across to the island. Colleen and Tucker had decided to take a walk on the beach, probably wanting some alone time. So Julie decided she might as well make herself useful by throwing away trash and taking down decorations.

"You don't have to do that. I know you must be tired. I'll take care of it," William said. She smiled when she thought about the attitude William had when he first showed up at her door that night. He and Dixie had forged a brand new relationship now, and it was really a miracle to witness.

"Oh, I don't mind. Gives me something to do." She pulled down some streamers that were hanging over her head and tossed them into the big garbage can beside her.

"Janine told me about you and Dawson breaking up. I'm sorry to hear that."

She wiped down a table before he folded it up. "All good things must come to an end."

"I hope not. Janine and I have a pretty good thing going." He winked at her and smiled.

"I guess old sayings don't always make a whole lot of sense."

"Janine didn't tell me why you broke up. Was it something in particular?"

"I'm just really busy right now with Meg and this whole thing, so I felt like taking a break was the best option."

"You know, Dawson's a great guy. He could be a wonderful support system for you with all of this. I don't want to butt my nose in your business, but I would tell you that he would never let you down."

She wanted to say something. She wanted to tell him that Dawson had already let her down. That he had been spending time with the high school beauty queen instead of her.

"Say, can I ask you something?"

"Sure."

"Do you remember a girl from high school named Tiffany. Blonde hair, dated a guy named Blaine?"

He chuckled. "Everybody at our high school knew Tiffany. She was kind of hard to miss. Big, bleached blonde hair, short miniskirts, legs that went on for miles…"

"Yes, so I've heard."

"Why do you ask?"

"She introduced herself to me at the reunion. I was just wondering if you knew her."

"Oh, yeah, most of the guys in our high school were walking around with their tongues hanging out after her. I thought she was pretty, but I never pursued anything."

"Dawson said she was his high school crush."

"Now I remember that. One time he cooked up a plan to ask her out on Valentine's Day, but she had her first date with Blaine. And then they ended up dating for the rest of high school. And then they apparently got married. But I heard through the grapevine that they divorced a year ago."

Julie's heart sank. That's why she was hanging around with Dawson. She was determined to put her hooks into him, and he was obviously falling for it. He certainly didn't look like he was being kept against his will.

"You know what? I am a little tired after all. If you don't need anything else, I might head home to check on Meg."

"Of course. Janine and I will be here for a while."

He looked over at her, laughing. "She hasn't stopped talking in the last two hours. I might have to drag her out of here so she can get up for her classes in the morning."

Julie smiled, waved at her sister and walked out the door. She just wanted to get home and drown her sorrows in a nice bowl of ice cream with cut up bananas and cherries on top. She might even dig out that hot fudge she saw in the cupboard the last time she needed to drown her sorrows.

# CHAPTER 11

*M*eg stood outside of Janine's yoga studio, staring through the window. She didn't know how her aunt had talked her into this. The class was for pregnant and new mothers, and it was supposed to be pretty gentle.

She had seen her aunt put herself in all kinds of positions, often looking like a human pretzel. She couldn't imagine a yoga class that wouldn't wear her out, but Janine had promised her that it would give her more energy and help get her pelvic floor in shape for childbirth. Meg didn't know exactly what that meant, but anything that would help her get through labor was a good plan in her book. She had been reading up about childbirth, and she had even been brave enough to watch a few videos. Now she wished she hadn't.

From what she could tell, childbirth looked more like a crime scene than a loving moment of bringing a baby into the world. She was definitely going to tell her doctor that she wanted all the drugs. Any drug they would give her. She didn't care what it was.

She remembered her grandmother telling her a long time ago that when she gave birth to Meg's mother, they knocked her out and she woke up with a baby in her arms. Meg didn't understand why they didn't still do things that way. It sure seemed like a much easier way to go about birthing a child.

"What are you doing out here?" Janine said, poking her head out the front door of the studio as she waved for Meg to come inside.

"I'm not sure I should try this. I've never done yoga in my life."

"I'll be gentle," Janine said, reaching out and pulling her niece through the doorway.

The place was pretty empty, although class didn't start for another ten minutes. Still, she expected there to be more students, rolling out their yoga mats and chanting or whatever it was that yogis did.

"Where is everybody?"

"Actually, this is a newer class, so I think I'm only going to have you and a couple of other students. They should be here shortly."

"Are they pregnant?"

"One of them is just a few weeks along, and the other one had her baby eight weeks ago. She's just now getting back into exercise and wants to tighten up her core muscles."

Meg looked down at her stomach. "I don't think I have core muscles anymore."

Janine laughed. "Don't worry. They're under there, and we're going to get them nice and strong before you give birth in a few weeks."

"Don't remind me. I'm pretty terrified about the whole thing."

Janine rolled out a yoga mat on the floor and grabbed a couple of foam blocks. She also gave Meg a hand towel and a bottle of water.

"This is all you should need for your first class. You may not even need those blocks, but just in case any of the poses are too difficult, you can use them for support."

The other two women walked in shortly after. One woman, apparently the one who was newly pregnant, only had a little tiny baby bump. Meg missed the time that she had those first few weeks when no one could really tell she was pregnant. If she didn't know this woman had a baby growing inside of her, she never would've assumed it.

But she was surprised when she saw the other

woman. She was pushing a stroller with a tiny baby inside, apparently asleep. But the girl didn't look much older than she was, if at all. She was definitely young. For a moment, Meg wondered if this was by design. Had Janine invited her to this class specifically to meet this woman?

"Welcome, everyone! I'm so glad you ladies can join us. I'd like to go around the room and have everyone introduce themselves."

They went around the room, and Meg learned that the woman's name was Casey. She was twenty years old, much like Meg, and was getting married in a few months. The baby was unexpected, which was more information than Meg thought someone should give when introducing themselves to a class full of strangers.

She sat down on the floor as Janine instructed in her opening remarks, and they began the class. There was a lot of breathing, slow stretching and the occasional pose that was more challenging. Meg was surprised that she was able to keep up.

When it was over, they laid on the floor in corpse pose, arms and legs spread out. Breathing in and out, Meg felt herself relaxing more than she had in months. Maybe this yoga thing was something she should add to her regular regimen. It definitely made her feel less stressed, and she felt muscles she forgot she had.

The newly pregnant woman left quickly after class, saying she had a doctor's appointment. But the other woman, Casey, hung around. Janine gushed over how cute the baby boy was.

"His name is Harrison," Casey said, beaming with pride.

"Well, little Harrison is adorable. I think he might be a movie star one day," Janine said, looking down at him.

Meg had often wondered if her aunt wished that she had children of her own. She never really talked about it, but Meg always thought she would've made a great mother.

"So, when are you due?" Casey asked her.

"Oh, not until mid summer."

"Not much longer now!"

"I guess you're right."

"So, I noticed we're around the same age. Pretty scary to think about raising a baby, isn't it?"

Meg smiled slightly. Janine asked to hold the baby, and Casey nodded. She walked across the room, rocking the sleeping infant back and forth in her arms.

"Yes. For me, it was not planned."

Casey laughed. "Mine wasn't planned either. But I have to say, he has been the greatest blessing of my life. It's hard. Don't get me wrong. Long nights, lots of messy diapers. But, the moment they put him on my chest, I knew he would be the great love of my life."

Meg's stomach knotted up. Would she want them to put the baby on her chest if she was giving it away? Could she live the rest of her life without ever holding her baby?

"If you ever want to meet for lunch or something, I could definitely use a friend in town. My boyfriend just got relocated here, so I don't know anyone. And I'd be glad to let you practice with my baby," Casey said, smiling.

"You know what, I don't have any friends here either. Maybe we could meet for lunch tomorrow?" She couldn't believe she was saying that. Meg had never been an overly friendly sort, opting out of most social engagements in order to read a book at home. But for some reason, she felt a kinship with this woman.

"That would be awesome. There's a great little sandwich shop over on Elm Street. Say, twelve-thirty tomorrow?"

"I'll see you there."

Janine walked over and handed the baby back to the woman who put him, still sleeping, in the stroller. As Meg watched them walk out the door, she was more sure than ever that her aunt had set the whole thing up, but for some reason she didn't care.

THE NEXT DAY, Meg met with Casey for lunch. She was surprised at how similar they were, and they got along like old friends. Casey had gone to college for almost two years before learning she was pregnant with her boyfriend's baby. They had gotten engaged shortly afterward, and their wedding was going to be at Christmas time.

Meg liked watching Casey's interaction with her infant son. She seemed comfortable, like she'd been taking care of babies her whole life.

"Did you do a lot of babysitting as a teenager?" Meg asked her, as she took a bite of her salad.

"Not really. I wasn't big into kids," Casey said, laughing as she burped Harrison over her shoulder.

"How did you learn how to take care of him so well? Did your mother help?"

Casey looked sad. "My mother isn't in my life. She's chosen alcohol and men over being a parent to me and my brother."

"I'm so sorry to hear that."

"I'm used to it. But, I'm determined to be the best mom in the world to my son. I don't want him to ever wonder if I love him or if I'm proud of him."

"Well, for what it's worth, you seem like a natural," Meg said.

"Thanks. I'll be honest. Those first couple of

weeks were hard. Really tough. My boyfriend and I were pretty lost. His mother was a big help, but when she went back to Florida, we were on our own. Tray, my boyfriend, had to go right back to work. So, I was left alone a lot of the time. I had to learn so much, but a lot of it comes naturally, you know? I mean, he's my kid, and I've known him since the moment he was conceived. There's a connection there I can't explain."

Meg thought about the connection she was already feeling with her child. Could she hand him or her over and never look back?

"I'm really nervous about the giving birth part."

Casey laughed. "It's no walk in the park, but the drugs they give you are fantastic. And once you have that baby in your arms, you forget all the pain you went through."

Suddenly, Meg began to cry. She hated crying, especially in front of a virtual stranger in public, but her emotions were all over the place.

"Oh, honey, are you okay?" Casey asked as she laid Harrison back in his stroller.

"No, I'm not. I've been thinking about adoption."

Casey paused for a moment. "Oh."

"I just don't know what to do. My boyfriend is here - he's from France - and wants to be a father. My Mom, aunt and sister are all here. Everyone wants to support me, but I'm trying to think of what's best for my child."

"Only you can decide that, Meg. But, I'll tell you what I think. Your child needs one thing - love. All of the other stuff will fall into place. You have a support system. I don't. And I'm still doing it. My baby is thriving, and I'm exhausted. But, I know it'll all be worth it."

JULIE WAS MORE than a little bit excited about hosting a surprise party for Meg. Janine was working on the finishing touches for the cake while she hung the decorations. It seemed like they'd done nothing but host parties for the last couple of weeks. It had been that long since she had seen Dawson, not that she was counting down the days or anything.

She had thought about inviting him to the party, but decided against it. Even though she had said she wanted to be his friend, it was far too painful to have him around. She thought time away would make her miss him less, but that wasn't happening. Sometimes, she thought that it had been easier to get over Michael than it was to get over Dawson.

Maybe that was because Michael had betrayed her in the most egregious way a husband can. Dawson, on the other hand, was still a good person.

A good man. And the person she thought was perfect for her.

At night, when she couldn't go to sleep, she considered calling him and just telling him what she had seen that day with him and Tiffany. Maybe there is a logical explanation, although she couldn't think of one. He was obviously hiding it from her, and that never had a good outcome.

But she was still having a hard time being angry at him. It seemed so against his nature to do what she thought he was doing. Risking her heart was something she just couldn't see herself doing again, even if it meant she had to be alone for the rest of her life.

"Ta-da!" Janine said, stepping back from the cake and holding her hands in the air. She had been insistent that she wanted to make Meg's birthday cake instead of buying it from the local bakery. Julie had thought it was funny because Janine had never been super good in the kitchen.

She walked over and looked. It was a double layer cake with white icing that had chocolate chips in it, Meg's favorite. When she was a kid, she would sit down on the kitchen floor with a spoon and a container of that icing and eat it all in one sitting. Of course, she always had the requisite stomach ache for a few hours after that. Being such a petite person, she had always been able to put away massive quantities of food and never gain any weight. Now that she was eating for two, it was strange to see her eat and gain weight. She had never been that big in her life.

There were only a few weeks left before she was going to give birth, and she still hadn't said a peep about her plans. Julie knew that she had met with the adoption attorney again, and she had at least looked through some more adoptive family files a couple of weeks ago. But other than that, she didn't seem to have made a final decision.

On the one hand, that gave Julie hope. But on the other hand, she felt like Meg might just be procrastinating on telling her family the final decision.

Today was about celebration. She was turning twenty years old, about to become a mother and they were going to have a good time no matter what.

Christian knocked on the front door and then entered. He had become more comfortable around the family, always chipping in to lend a helping hand at whatever they were working on.

"Allow me to help you there," he said, reaching up with his long arms to help Julie hang the last of the decorations. His French accent had become endearing to her, although sometimes he said words she couldn't understand. They had taught him to say "y'all" and "down yonder", which was hysterical to hear coming out of his mouth.

"So, where is Meg?" Janine asked.

"I had Colleen take her to do some more maternity shopping since she can barely fit into those shorts we bought her. They should be here any minute, though. Colleen texted me when they were checking out at the store."

Dixie, William and Meg's new friend, Casey, all arrived at the same time. Everybody had pulled their cars down the road to a neighbor's house who had agreed to allow them to park there. Meg should have no idea this was going on.

"She's going to be so surprised," Julie said, a broad smile on her face.

"Yes, she is," Janine said. They all waited in the hallway as they saw Colleen pull into the driveway. When they walked through the door, the whole group came running out of the hallway screaming surprise. Meg put her hand to her heart.

"Oh my gosh! Y'all nearly scared me half to death! I'm surprised I didn't go into labor early!"

Everybody laughed and took turns hugging her.

"Happy birthday, sweetie!" Julie said, hugging her daughter's neck tightly.

"Thanks, Mom. I can't believe you did this!"

Meg walked over to Christian, who leaned down and pecked her on the lips. Their relationship seemed to be progressing day by day. Christian was getting close to starting his new job, and he had found a small apartment on the mainland.

"Thank you all for coming! It means the world to me to be turning twenty years old and have so many wonderful friends and family around me."

They spent the next hour eating appetizers, cake and ice cream. As they sang to Meg around the lit candle, Julie wondered what her wish would be. Would she wish for guidance on what to do about the baby? Would she wish for a great job or to win the lottery? Julie always wondered what people wished when they blew out their candles.

As the party was wrapping up, Meg had a look on her face that Julie couldn't identify. She seemed stressed, anxious about something.

"Everybody, can I have your attention?" Meg said, standing up. "I want to say thank you to everyone for coming. I only have a few weeks left of this pregnancy, and I have to say that I didn't expect to be pregnant when I was this age. But, I'm also aware that every baby is a blessing. I know that a lot of you have wondered what I'm going to do about the baby. It's been a very long, difficult pregnancy, physically and emotionally."

Julie sat there, her hands sweating in her lap. What was this all about?

"I've gone back-and-forth in my mind a lot about whether to pursue adoption because I want my baby to have the best life possible. I want him or her to have everything they need, and to have all the love in the world. So I've struggled this whole time wondering if I could provide that. I've been wondering if I would be a good mother at all."

Julie swallowed hard. This didn't sound good. She and Janine had tried so hard over the last couple of months to show Meg that she had the support system she needed, but in the end, it came down to her decision.

"And what I've realized through all of this is that none of the families I've seen in the file folders can give my baby what this family can."

Julie sat there, stunned. Was she hearing what she thought she was?

"Family is about love, and while I'm sure those families have a lot of love, they can't match the love I have for this baby. And I know that love isn't enough. That's where support comes in. And there's no family in the world that could have the support that I do. From my mom," she said, pointing to Julie. "To my aunt Janine and my sister. And to this wonderful man standing beside me." She looked up at Christian, and he smiled. "And now I have a new friend and fellow mother, Casey, to help me along as well."

"Honey, are you saying that you're going to keep the baby?" Julie asked, her hands in prayer position under her chin. Janine reached over and squeezed her leg, the two of them teary-eyed.

"I'm going to keep my baby!"

The entire crowd erupted in celebratory screams, each of them running over and hugging Meg yet again.

"So," she said, trying to calm down the hoots and hollers happening in the room. "I thought now would be as good a time as any to do a gender reveal."

"Oh, how fun!" Janine said, clapping her hands together.

Meg walked across the room to her purse, and reached inside to pull out an envelope. Janine recognized it from the doctor's appointment.

"That's where the ultrasound technician wrote the gender," she said.

"Yes, it is. So I thought I could open it, and let all of us know what kind of baby clothes we need to be looking for!"

"I can't wait to find out what we're having," Christian said, watching Meg tear the envelope open.

She pulled out the paper and stared at it for a moment, a smile spreading across her face.

"Well, Casey, tell Harrison to get ready because his future wife is coming soon!"

Julie and Janine jumped up and down, holding

each other's hands. "A baby girl!" they said simultaneously.

As everyone celebrated and talked about the baby for the first time, Julie couldn't help but smile from ear to ear. Her cheeks would definitely be hurting tomorrow.

# CHAPTER 12

*D*awson stood at the water's edge, tossing seashells he found on his walk back into the ocean. He'd done that since he was a kid, rarely ever bringing shells back to the house with him. His grandmother had explained when he was young that seashells were homes for living creatures in the ocean, so he always felt bad about keeping them.

Today, his mind was elsewhere. He'd heard through the grapevine, a.k.a. Dixie, that Meg had chosen to keep the baby. He'd also heard all about the birthday party and the gender reveal, and while he was happy for Julie and her family, he felt excluded.

Much to his dismay, he'd made plans in his mind about a future with Julie and her whole family. He had seen himself there, when he was old and gray, chasing grandchildren right alongside her. It was the first time since losing his wife that he had visions of the future that made him happy.

But it was over. And he still really didn't understand why.

He sat down in the sand, digging his feet into the warmth, and stared out into the open water. This place had always brought him serenity, but sometimes he looked out and it made him miss Julie. Even though she had claimed they could be friends, he felt like she had cut him out of her life.

"Hey, man," William said, walking up behind him.

"Oh, hey. Didn't expect to see you out here."

William was carrying a fishing pole. "Oh, I had a day off so I just thought I would do some fishing in the surf. You don't mind, do you?"

"Of course not. My beach is your beach."

As William got his pole set up, he looked over at Dawson.

"You okay?"

"Yeah."

"Because you don't look okay," he said, sitting down next to his friend.

"Just lost in thought, I guess."

"About Julie?"

"I guess."

"I know what it's like to be in an argument with the woman you love. Sorry, man."

Dawson sighed. "That's the thing. I could deal with an argument. This isn't an argument. She's just completely broken things off with me, and I have no idea why."

"You know, she asked me some questions the other day that were kind of weird."

"What kind of questions?" Dawson asked, looking at him.

"Well, we were cleaning up after Janine's party, and she was asking me if I knew Tiffany from high school."

Dawson looked at him quizzically. "Tiffany? Why on earth would she be asking about her?"

"No clue. It was strange."

"What did you tell her?"

"I just told her how all the guys were in love with Tiffany, and about that time you were going to ask her out for Valentine's Day but she ended up dating Blaine. Then I told her I heard that Tiffany had gotten divorced recently."

Dawson sat there for a long moment. Could that conversation have anything to do with why Julie wanted to break up with him? Surely not. She would have at least asked him about it.

He continued looking out over the water. What would make her ask about Tiffany? Why would she even care?

One thing is for sure, he would never understand

women.

～

JULIE WALKED THROUGH THE SHOP, giddy with delight about shopping for her new granddaughter. She was so thrilled that Meg had made the decision to keep the baby, and now she had to play catch-up buying all the stuff.

They had talked over the last few days about where they would live, the nursery and all of the other important things one must think about when having a baby.

They came to the decision that Meg would continue living with her mother, carving out a small nursery area in her bedroom. Colleen had decided to get an apartment on the mainland, not because she didn't want to be with her family, but because she wanted to start establishing her own life. She was an adult, and it was time for her to move out and find her own place.

Julie had made sure she didn't feel pushed out, and she said she didn't. She wanted to be closer to work, although she was intent on finding a new job soon.

Meg and Christian had already found a great crib at a consignment store. He was helping her design another nursery at his new apartment in the spare bedroom. She was going to split her time back-and-forth until they figured out their relationship. Julie thought they would certainly get married, but Meg didn't want to make a decision until after the baby. She wanted to make sure it was for love, and not obligation, that she and Christian were getting married. Plus, she said, she wanted the whole big wedding with a much smaller wedding dress than the one she could wear now.

As she looked through the racks of clothing, she picked up every girly, frilly, pink thing she could find. Of course, there was always the chance that the baby wouldn't be a girly girl, but until she could make those decisions for herself, Julie was determined to dress her like a beauty queen.

She paid for her purchases and walked out of the store, a smile on her face. She was going to be a grandmother soon, and she couldn't wait.

She had sat by her daughter the night before when Meg had finally called and told her father about the pregnancy. At first, he was really upset that he didn't know until she was just a few weeks away from delivering. Eventually, he forgave everyone for keeping it from him and got really excited that he was going to be a grandfather. He would be coming to town soon to see Meg and meet Christian.

Julie tried not to think about the fact that

RACHEL HANNA

Victoria would be considered the baby's grandmother too. She just couldn't go there in her mind
right now.

She walked down to the bookstore to relieve
Dixie who had a doctor's appointment. She put her
bags behind the counter and tried to get herself back
in the mindset to work. Tourist season was in full
gear, and the store was busy from opening to
closing.

When she heard the bell ring, she didn't expect to
look up and see Tiffany walking into the store. She
had hoped maybe the woman had left town, but no
such luck.

"Good afternoon. Is there something I can help
you with?" Julie said, gritting her teeth and trying to
smile.

Tiffany, her hair bigger than Julie had ever seen
it, smiled that fake, toothy white smile of hers.

"I'm looking for a book about traveling to
Australia. I'm going to be taking a trip next year, and
I want to learn all about it."

"Our travel section is in the back on the right."

Tiffany started to walk to the back of the store,
but then stopped and turned around. She looked at
Julie carefully.

"Don't I know you from somewhere?"

"We met at the reunion."

"Oh, that's right. Dawson's girlfriend."

"Right," Julie said, not wanting to correct her.

"You're a lucky lady. He's a very handsome man."

"Yes, he is."

She started to walk again, but turned around one more time.

"You know, I hope he told you that I didn't mean to cause any harm."

"What?"

"I mean, yes, I might have thrown myself at him a bit while he was doing the renovations on my new house. But I didn't know y'all were that serious until Dawson got mad at me. I thought you were just a date he brought to the reunion."

"I don't know what you're talking about. Reno-vations?"

"Yes, Dawson renovated a little fixer-upper I bought to flip for profit. I've been in town for the last few weeks, and he was working on my house."

"Oh, I didn't know that."

"Yes, and I think I might've driven him a little bit crazy. He got mad at me a few times during that process, but we finished up last week, and the house is already in escrow."

"So you're leaving?"

"Yes. I got quite a settlement from my divorce and a lot of money from this house, so I'm going to do some world traveling. Look for a beautiful man with an accent," she said, giggling like a schoolgirl.

So, Dawson hadn't been cheating on her with Tiffany. He had been working on her house, probably not wanting to tell Julie so she wouldn't be jealous or worried.

She felt like the world's biggest fool. Would he even forgive her?

Now, she felt a bit like a trapped animal, caught in the cage of the bookstore, unable to leave until they closed. She wanted to run straight to Dawson and apologize for being a jerk.

"You have a good man there. Don't let him go," Tiffany said before going to look at books.

Julie wondered if that advice was a bit too late.

JULIE DROVE over the bridge to the island, going a lot faster than she normally would. For some reason, it felt like time was ticking away, like if she didn't get to Dawson soon, she would explode.

Her mind raced as she wondered if he would forgive her. Would he understand why she had done what she did?

She pulled into his driveway, his truck sitting there, as expected.

She jumped out of her car and ran up to the front door, knocking frantically. He was probably going to think she was insane.

Lucy opened the door. "Oh, hello, Miss Julie. How can I help you?"

"Hi, Lucy. Is Dawson around?"

"Oh, honey, he's down on the beach. He's been spending a lot of time down there lately."

The sun was just starting to set, so Julie opted to walk down there and try to find him. She thanked Lucy and jogged toward the beach.

When she got down there, she found Dawson, a small fire going beside him in the fire pit. He was sitting in a chair, staring out over the horizon, watching the sun set.

She stopped for a moment and stood there. What was she going to say? What if he told her he didn't want to get back together? What if she wasn't worth all this hassle?

For a moment, she thought about turning around and going back to her car. Maybe it was better to just leave things alone. Maybe she didn't deserve a great man like him.

Sensing someone was behind him, he turned around.

"Julie?"

She stood there, like she was frozen with her feet in quicksand.

"Hey."

He stood up slowly, not walking toward her, but instead standing there, his hands in his pockets.

"What are you doing here?"

"I'm so sorry. I was so wrong."

"What?"

"I thought you were cheating on me with Tiffany."

His eyes opened wide, his mouth hanging open. "How on earth could you think that?"

She was finally able to make her feet move, so she slowly walked closer. "I saw you exchange cards at the reunion, and then one day I saw you coming out of a restaurant together."

He laughed and shook his head. "And that made you think I was cheating on you? What kind of man do you think I am?"

She shrugged her shoulders. "I thought my husband was a loyal, good man."

He shook his head. "I can't take the blame for your husband's sins. I'm not the same guy that he is.

"I know that now."

She took a few steps closer.

"I thought you would've already known that," he said, sadly.

"Tiffany came into the bookstore today. She let it slip that she had made some moves on you while you were renovating her house. Why didn't you just tell me you were doing that job?"

"Because I didn't want you to worry. I didn't want

you to even have to think about it with everything you had going on."

"She told me that you got mad when she made a pass at you."

He nodded his head. "Because when a man is in love and loyal, he doesn't put up with that sort of thing, Julie. No other woman can hold a candle."

Love? They hadn't said those words to each other yet. She stared at him . "Wait. You love me?"

He finally started to walk toward her, a smile on his face. "Yes, I love you. Do you love me?"

She let out the breath she had been holding. "Of course, I love you."

"Then why are you fighting so hard to mess this whole thing up?"

"I guess I wanted to hurt you before you could hurt me."

He walked over and put his hands on her cheeks, looking down into her eyes. "Well, you definitely hurt me."

"I'm really sorry. I was an idiot."

"Well, you're my idiot," he said, leaning down and kissing her.

"So you forgive me?"

"Of course I do. But, please don't ever doubt me again. Talk to me. Ask me."

"Agreed."

"There is no other woman I would want in my

life, Julie. And especially not Tiffany. That woman is a nightmare. God bless the man that ends up with her."

Julie laughed. "I'm so glad to be here with you right now."

"Ditto."

He pulled her back over to the chair, and she sat on his lap, his arms around her waist as they stared and watched the sun set together. She never felt so at home in her life.

"So, I hear you're going to be a grandma?" Julie squealed with delight. This was going to be the best time of her life. She just knew it.

# EPILOGUE

*J*ulie wished she could do something. As Meg screamed and pushed, the baby didn't seem to be budging a bit. Finally, the doctor made the call for a c-section, mostly due to Meg's tiny stature. The baby just couldn't come out the natural way.

As she paced in the waiting room, Dawson tried to soothe her. She'd been up all night, ever since Christian had called and said that Meg had gone into labor. She'd been staying at his new apartment as the due date approached, mainly because it was close to the hospital and made Meg feel more at ease.

"I hope everything's okay in there," Julie said, craning her head for the hundredth time to look at the swinging doors they wheeled Meg through over an hour before.

"I'm sure it's fine, Mom. The doctors do this all the time," Colleen said. Tucker sat beside her, furiously drawing on his tablet, probably designing a new toy.

Colleen had quit her job a week ago, opting to take a newly formed position at Tucker's company. She was handling intellectual property for them, and it made Julie happy to see that Colleen had finally found something she loved to do. Of course, working with Tucker also seemed like something she loved.

Janine walked back into the waiting room with William, both of them holding cups of coffee.

"Here ya go. Cream and extra sugar," she said, handing it to Julie. "And for Dawson, black and manly," she said in a deep voice.

Dawson laughed. "Puts hair on your chest if you drink it black."

"You don't need more hair on your chest," William said, smacking him on the shoulder.

"Anybody want a cookie?" Dixie asked, pulling out a container full of fresh baked chocolate chip cookies she'd brought. She never went anywhere without sweet treats to share.

"No, thanks. I'm keyed up enough without chocolate and sugar," Julie said, looking down the hallway again.

"Honey, please sit down," Dawson pleaded again.

"I can't. That's my baby in there. What if something goes wrong?"

"Are you Julie Pike?" a nurse asked as she walked around the corner.

"Yes, that's me."

"Your daughter asked me to come get you."

"Is she okay?"

The woman smiled. "Absolutely. She and the baby are doing just fine. Would you like to come see her?"

"Yes!"

"Come with me."

Julie grinned and waved at her friends and family before following the nurse. They walked down the hallway and turned down another one before stopping in front of a door.

"She's right in there."

Julie slowly opened the door, poking her head inside. She saw Meg, exhaustion on her face, lying in bed. She was holding the tiniest bundle of joy against her bare skin. Julie could hear the sounds that newborns make, and her heart melted.

"How're you doing?" she asked.

"I'm tired, but I'm so thankful. She's amazing, Mom."

Julie walked to her bedside and saw her granddaughter's face for the first time. She looked like an angel. Her big blue eyes were open wide like she was taking in everything she could.

"She's beautiful, Meg. Oh my goodness. My heart is so full."

Christian stood on the other side of the bed, his face beaming with pride as he looked down at his daughter. Julie felt so much love as she witnessed the new little family.

"I had Christian call Dad. He should be here soon."

"Good. He's going to be thrilled to meet... Wait, what's her name?"

Meg smiled. "Genevieve Olivia Bisset. She'll have Christian's last name."

"Genevieve?"

"It means 'God's blessing' in French," she said, smiling down at her daughter. "We'll call her Vivi."

"It's perfect."

It was all perfect. As Julie watched her daughter with her own daughter now, it felt like a full circle moment. Her daughters had both grown into strong women, and maybe they wouldn't need her as much anymore. But, now she had a granddaughter who would.

Life hadn't always been perfect, and she had taken some curveballs to the head at times, but the destination was better than anything she could've imagined on her own.

WANT to find out what happens next on Seagrove Island? Download the next book in this series by clicking HERE to get your copy of THE INN AT SEAGROVE.

Looking for a really fun book to read? Check out WISTERIA ISLAND. A woman running from a humiliating moment in her life, a wealthy businessman and an island full of misfit old people!

Be sure to order book 1 in my other new series, SWEET TEA B&B! This is a women's fiction story focused on two sisters who don't know the other exists, but are forced together to run their late mother's B&B in the north GA mountains. You'll love it!

If you loved this book, you might want to also dig into my January Cove series. It's set in a little beach town too! Read book one by clicking HERE.

Want to find out about all of my new releases! You can get on my VIP reader list by clicking HERE.

Made in United States
Orlando, FL
17 March 2022

15893703R10107